FIXED PARTS

PARTS OF ME SERIES, BOOK 2

J. A. WYNTERS

Fixed Parts, Parts of Me series, Book 2

Editing by: Sarah Villanueva at Dear Jane Editing

Cover design: Jo- Anne Walker

Interior Formatting: Dawn Lucous, Yours Truly Book Services

This one is for Lauren - for all the right and wrong reasons - I love you.

You are about to start a long journey spanning FIVE books. If you buy this ticket and board this freight train, prepare for it to be a long and bumpy ride as we delve into all the uncomfortable parts of life. These may trigger some readers so be sure you want to get on. These books will end on cliffhangers, have twists and turns and this train is sure to be derailed as it enters a long dark tunnel of depravity.

YOU HAVE BEEN WARNED.

Adult themes, strong language, graphic scenes. Enter at your own risk.

PART VIII

othing screams at you louder than silence.

I woke up. My face, pinned against the white door, felt bruised and sore. I wasn't six anymore, and Alice wasn't on the other side.

No one was.

I remained slumped against the door. My back ached from sleeping in a seated position. I felt parched; I should have left.

But I couldn't stay away.

I wanted to...

I needed to...

I wanted *her*.

I needed *her*.

I knew I shouldn't have stayed, but I was consumed. Possessed. Desperate.

I kept waiting.

I waited until my stomach grumbled, and the sun shifted across the horizon colouring the walls in yellows and oranges.

I waited as life moved around me in slow motion. People

moved on with their lives, while I sat at her doorstep with withered wings and a splintered soul.

I watched the clouds move across the sky, cars rolling by, and dogs sniffing at trees.

I waited till the sky fell black and the smell of dinner wafted from beneath doors and oozed into the street. And when she still hadn't shown, I crossed the road to the phone booth and called Salvatore.

The phone rang once before he picked up.

"It's me."

"What do you need, boss?"

"First, I need you to stop calling me that," He huffed. "Then I need you to find Mia. She's not at her place, she didn't come back last night, and she hasn't shown all day."

There was hesitant silence on the other end of the line. "What do you want me to do with her when I find her?"

"Just let me know where she is." My body hummed with tension.

"And that's all?"

"That's all." I heard the sharp exhale.

"Consider her found." The line went dead.

My mind felt broken.

Shattered.

My body felt heavy, which was strange given how empty I felt.

I slumped into my car seat, and the engine roared to life. I shot Mia's apartment one final glance, then took off.

When the mind is in pain, it finds anchors to latch onto; small things in each day to make it more bearable, survivable—small, achievable tasks.

I didn't know how long I had been staring at the gaskets

but, when I moved away, my palm felt warm as if I had been grasping it for a while.

My mind kept slipping to the first time Alice disappeared. The fear. The coiled stomach and cold fingers, the tightening of everything.

The wait.

The agonised minutes and hours.

These days, I was used to Alice disappearing—it was just what she did.

But Mia?

Where the fuck was Mia?

•

Mia had been gone for a week and the unknown gnawed at me. Salvatore remained silent; no answers, no Mia. Was I going to find her like they found Rita? I slammed the bonnet shut and trudged to my room, slamming the door behind me. The boys would take care of the cars; I needed to take care of business.

I felt stiff.

Stiff from anger I couldn't shake, stiff from desire I couldn't quench, stiff with worry that wouldn't settle.

My body shook as I fought the urge to throw everything around the room, to fight the white walls till they bled. Instead, I discarded my work clothes and dressed in something more comfortable. I called for Spots, and we ran.

The wind whipped against my face, pushing itself into my burning lungs, forcing me to breathe, to inhale, to clear my mind and focus. My feet pounded the pavement, and Spots' paws clipped against the road as he bounded behind me. With every heartbeat, hot blood rushed through my body, pushing the choice from my heart to my brain, forcing me to accept the inevitable. I kept running, running from ghosts of the past and into the arms of the monsters that waited on the other side.

The sun was somewhere between hanging low and sinking. Indecisive. Unsure of its place. Just like me. It knew its path, but it hung on a little bit longer, resisting, fighting. Fighting the pull, the force, the burning course that has been carved out for it. It was losing the battle when we reached the garage.

I panted, sucking in deep lungfuls of air, as I pushed through the door. Sweat burned my eyes and leaked down my face. I stroked away the beads, listening. The office phone rang. It buzzed like an annoyed insect in the silence of the garage. I took the steps two at a time and grabbed the receiver.

"She's at Stephano's." His voice was calm.

The breath left my body in a sharp exhale, "Thanks." I hung up.

It was going to be a long night.

⚜

The junk yard was a wasteland where things went to die. Cars, evidence, people, it was easy to get lost in the chaos. The rusted, corrugated iron gates hung open, and I took a step inside. Spots tottered in behind me. The muddied path enclosed on both sides with dead and emptied husks of rusting cars waiting for their end in the crusher.

Like an ogre in a swamp, Stephano's office sat in the middle of the mud. He was surrounded by filth and dangerous as hell.

His house stood a few hundred meters beyond. It was an oddity that stuck out amid all the rotting, teetering piles. The house was whitewashed, enclosed by a lush green garden that ran up to a wooden porch surrounding the exterior. A bench swing nested in the corner. It would have been idyllic if it wasn't for Mia sitting on the swing with another man. My eyes narrowed as I watched him slither his arm over her shoulder and whisper in her ear. She smiled and he slid closer to her. I ground my teeth at my stupidity. White-hot fury washed over me as I watched him leer over her, his fiery hair alight in the sunlight. I was going to kill that man. But not yet.

I resisted the urge to run to her, to call for her. She smiled at the man again, and my fists clenched, nails digging into my palm. If she would only look up.

My feet squelched along the path as I made my way towards the wooden office. With every step, I could feel eyes on me. I couldn't see them, but I knew they were there. The door to the office flew open, and Stefano stepped out. A cigarette dangling from his mouth. He leaned on the door frame, sucking in black tar and blowing out white smoke.

"Stephano, long time no see." My heart rattled in my chest, constricting with anger. *Mia, Mia, Mia.* It beat.

"Hello, you piece of shit." He exhaled the words with a puff of white smoke.

"Nice to see you, too."

I smiled at the man, and he leered at me in return.

"How can I help you, Gabriel?"

I stepped closer and swivelled my head a little in each direction to see two men flanking me on each side. My eyes flashed over to the porch. That was a mistake. Carrot Top was way too close to Mia, snug if you will. Anger surged to the surface and pulsed underneath my skin, vibrating like its own living thing, as if it had its own will.

I cleared my throat trying to calm the surging storm inside me, "I heard Mia was staying over, I have her final paycheque."

In truth, I didn't have to be there, I wanted to be there. I was desperate to see her; my body remembered hers with dangerous, agonising longing, fuelled by a selfish need to possess and own her. The last paycheque was as good of an excuse as any. I didn't expect to find her in the arms of another man—the thought of it burned under my skin.

"She's a big girl, she could have picked it up Monday."

I shrugged, "What can I say? I thought I'd be a gentleman and save her the trouble."

"Is that why she's been hiding from you for a week? 'Cause you're a *gentleman*? What the fuck did you do to her?"

"Nothing she didn't want to do. She's an adult, she knew what she was getting into."

"Nobody fucking knows what they're getting into when it comes to you."

Stephano's stooges closed the distance around me. Spots stood beside me baring his teeth, his head swinging from man to man.

"Down boy," I soothed Spots when a glint of metal caught my eye. Stephano laughed as he pulled out a Glock and pointed it at Spots.

"No!" Fear crept up my spine. Memories barraging my brain like bullets.

"Where is your other dog? Salvatore? Too busy burying himself inside one of his bitches?" he laughed.

I bent down and took Spots' face in my palms. "Spots, go home buddy." He looked into my eyes. The big brown pools asking questions, trying to comprehend. I could see the hesitation flicker in his mind. He wanted to protect me, it was his job, so why was I pushing him away?

His head flinched away from my palm and twisted backwards with a snap, but it was too late. Stephano was already too close. The kick was fierce and brutal. Spots howled, the agony sending my heart into a frenzy. Spots pulled up his bad leg and it curled into his belly like it used to. My fists curled around Spots' fur, and they ached to wipe the smirk from Stephano's face.

"Please buddy," I begged, "Just go I'll be fine." Spots' eyes flickered with guilt and confusion. I nodded at him and he limped away, looking back at me. As the three men closed the space around me, he slunk away. I breathed in relief once he was safely behind the gates. I searched the porch for Mia and her mystery man. They were both gone.

"You didn't have to do that," I hissed through clenched teeth as I looked down at the barrel that was edging its way closer to my face with each of Stephano's wild swings. "I just came to hand over Mia's paycheque." Maybe if I said it out loud enough times, I would start believing it too.

"Like I said, you've wasted your time."

"What's it to you? Just let me conclude my business with your cousin, and I'll leave her be."

He smirked and dropped his cigarette into the mud, the orange ember hissed as it touched the water, "I don't think she wants to see you."

"I think she can make up her own mind about that." I tried to step out of the circle of men, but they tightened around me.

"Yeah? Well, she's been holed up at my house for a fucking week crying her eyes out. So, I ask you again, what did you do to her?"

My heart sank like an anchor in a pool of pain and guilt. I made her feel all those things—all the things I didn't want her to feel, "I didn't do anything."

I raked a hand through my hair. If she knew about Rita, would she understand? About Spots? Why couldn't she just leave it alone—me, us? Why couldn't I get her out of my fucking head? Why did every breath I took feel like it was burning in my chest and killing me slowly when she wasn't with me?

Stephano's weasel face sneered at me. His slim body twisted, and his fist connected with my face. The pain took a few seconds to register. It sank deep and hot and angry across my jaw. I had no time to breathe, no time to recover as Stephano's men lunged.

I dodged to the right and spun as their meaty hands reached for me. I threw my body weight behind my fist and slammed it into the man on my right, while a fist from the left sank into my stomach. I gagged for a second then dove at the other man; his eyes narrowed with determination as his fist whizzed by my head, missing me by mere inches.

I swung for a second time; my blood hummed in my veins as adrenaline coursed inside me. Pain blazed up my arm as my fist connected with his jaw, blood pooled in his mouth.

A blow smashed against my back, and the air huffed out of my lungs. I stumbled into the arms of the man I had just punched. He grabbed my head between his hands and slammed it forcefully into his kneecap.

Sharp, punishing pain burst inside my head, and my vision exploded. I stumbled backwards feeling hot liquid pour from my nose.

"Is that all you got?" I smirked, blood leaking into my mouth, coating my chin, and dripping into the mud in steady, angry droplets.

The goon drew his fist back and ploughed it into my stomach. It felt as though I had been hit by a freight train, my innards smashed together, blood vessels bursting, screaming. I fell to my knees; shallow breaths barely filled my lungs.

"Enough of this shit," Stephano crowed, producing his gun and holding it to my temple. The cold steel pushed against my throbbing head. "Let's finish this."

At his words, I tilted my head, my legs ready to lunge. Stephano swung the gun around, the butt smashing into my temple with such ferocity that my body crumpled. Stars burst in my vision, and my body felt limp. Hands gripped me, pulled at me, twisted, and tore.

I wanted to fight, but my body wouldn't respond. Everything felt heavy as I sank into the mud. Strong hands gripped my wrists and a knee pushed into my back, forcing my face into the shallow, dirty puddle. I gurgled as I tried to breathe, sucking in earth and putrid water.

I was helpless. Stephano's face twisted in a self-satisfied grin as he undid his pants and pulled out his dick.

It was the heat I felt first as it hit my neck, then flowed onto my head, coating my hair and face. His piss stung and burned my eyes as he emptied himself above me. He cackled as he pissed, a maniacal crazy laugh. He tucked himself back in and nodded. The weight lifted from my body, and I sucked in a sour, stinking breath.

The first blow was less painful than I anticipated; although, I knew it was only the first in a series that would only get more brutal, more savage. My body was wracked with pain as kick after kick landed from all three men. A barrage of strikes hit me from every direction.

Every part of my body gushed with pain. I could taste metal as blood oozed from my nose and into my mouth. My futile attempts at fighting depleted what was left of my energy.

Just as suddenly as it began, the beating ended. I tried to breathe; each dragging breath jarring and brutal as my chest panged with the effort. My right eye was clamped shut and the left was swelling up. My body pulsed and throbbed with red, raw currents of pain.

"Not so smart now, are you?" Stephano hissed and stepped back admiring his handy work. He pulled out his box of cigarettes and lit up, blowing out a white cloud of poison. I gagged on the puddle of piss and blood as it trickled leisurely down my throat.

Stephano closed the distance between us, squatted and grabbed my chin. Two claw-like, stained fingers clutched my jaw, digging into my flesh. He lifted my head and twisted my neck so that I could see his face with my left eye.

"Now listen here, you piece of shit. In case I haven't made myself clear, stay away from Mia." He sucked in a long drag and blew the smoke in my face, the noxious cloud suffocating.

"I keep telling her the same thing. Maybe she's the one with the problem." My voice was hoarse and strangled. I tried to smile but I barely managed a grimace. His fingers slipped away from my chin, and the back of his hand connected with my face. Blood pooled in my mouth, and I spit out the thick liquid. It exploded across Stephano's face. His eyes flickered with disdain, and his weasel smile returned. He swiped at the blood with the back of his hand, smearing it across his face like war paint.

"You've been warned."

With that, he turned his back to me and strolled towards his office, his two goons following suit.

"Stephano," I gurgled.

The men ignored me as I called out again. The door to the office slammed violently behind them. Somewhere a machine came to life, the angry engine burying all other noise. I remained in the puddle, straining against the mud. I tried to push myself up, but my arms were numb and my body a shell of pain.

Through the fog, I could see him; a fuzzy shape that grew clearer as he approached. "Spots?"

Spots circled around me, his feet sinking into the stained mud. He whimpered and pushed his nose into my face. I winced at his affection and he fell back, his tail tucked between his legs.

He whined; a forlorn sound from somewhere deep inside him. Despite the lancing pain in my body, his terror sliced me deeper. "It's alright, buddy. I'll be alright. Go home," I whispered, the last of my energy leaching from my body. Heaviness blanketed me and exhaustion wrapped itself around me. The world turned dark.

Urgent, worried voices pierced the darkness.
A distant hum.
A flash of light.
My arms felt weightless.
A sad, tortured whimper.
Shouting.
A streak of black hair and blue eyes.
Darkness.

A muffled whimper.
I tried to pry my eyes open, but they felt as if they were glued shut. My head felt heavy, disconnected.

Vicious pain sliced through the plump swelling of my face; I wanted to scream but the noise died in my throat.

Voices swam in the fog.

"There, that will help with the swelling."

"What is it?"

"It's cream. It helps with hematomas."

"English, doc."

"It'll take the swelling down tonight…"

More incoherent words, as pain pounded around my body—like a red hot poker prodding me. All I could do was breathe, even if it hurt.

The voices returned as the pain waned.

"…internal bleeding. You really need to get him to a hospital."

"That won't be necessary, doc." A deep, familiar voice.

"Well in that case, I'm afraid there's not…"

Something soft, familiar. A cold wetness on my palm, followed by hot breath.

Darkness.

A fragment of light slithered beyond my eyelid.
Light.

I sighed, blinking at the exquisite sensation of sight. I lay on my bed and inhaled slow, deep breaths, letting sensation sink in around me. My body throbbed in hot, deep agony. When it waned a little, I tried to sit up. Sharp pain lanced through my head, and stars collided behind my eyes. My body protested each movement, and I sucked in air in shallow gulps that burned my lungs. They must've broken a couple of ribs. From the corner of my eye, I caught movement. Spots leapt up from his bed, wagging his tail wildly.

"Hey, boy." I smiled at him and he galloped onto the bed, ploughing into me. I winced and curled, clasping my abdomen. He froze and whined. "I'm okay buddy, don't worry. Just be gentle."

He jumped off the bed and sat by my feet. Waiting. Staring. His big, watery eyes scrutinising me. He knew I was lying, that I wasn't anywhere near ok.

I stood up. My head spun as I limped to the bathroom, every step felt like daggers in my abdomen—my limbs feeling heavy, uncooperative.

I stood in front of the mirror and assessed the damage. Both of my eyes were bloodshot; two red balls staring out from half open lids, swollen and bruised. Dry blood caked my upper lip, which was splintered with a deep, maroon fissure that sliced through the plump skin. Purple marks decorated my body like sprinkles on a cupcake, except there was nothing sweet or delicious about this—it was all painful and agonising. The bruising would only deepen over the week.

I found comfort in the shower. The water cascaded over my skin, washing away cold blood and hot pain. Watering down the thick, murky feeling of Mia's frivolity. I inhaled a long, deep breath and took stock of myself. I winced at the pain each time I bent or flexed, stretching against the will of my joints. My skin felt lumpy where it should have been smooth. But Mia in the arms of another left a hollow ache inside me that almost matched the brutal pain spread across my body. I blinked away water and stepped out of the shower.

Spots didn't leave my side. He stayed by me as I showered and dressed, as I sat on my bed and sucked in deep, long breaths, and again when I stepped out of my room.

Salvatore was pacing outside my bedroom door. His usual chiselled face furrowed with deep crevices. He spun around, straightening up as he saw me.

"Hey boss, how are you feeling?"

"I've told you not to fucking call me that."

"I guess he must be feeling better." He looked to Spots.

"How did I get here?"

"Spots. He was running outside like a feral thing; his legs were covered in mud and blood…"

I nodded. "How long have I been out?"

"A day and a half. The doctor gave you something to help you sleep through the pain," he looked tired. Worn. "Do I need to go take care of it?" the lines in his forehead deepened, his eyes clouded.

"No, this was personal. It wasn't business."

His eyebrows rose a notch, "Are your sure, boss?"

"Yes." I watched the tension seep from his face, but the worry remained.

"Would you like me to stick around?"

"Go home, I'll be alright."

He seemed to hesitate for a second. His lip twitched, then he nodded, "I'm just a phone call away."

"Thank you." We exchanged something that was more than just a look. A thousand words were spoken between us, words of gratitude and respect. He tipped his head and headed for the door.

Once he was gone, I grabbed the phone and called Romeo. I told him to take the week off and to tell the other boys to do the same. He didn't argue, just asked if he'd be paid. Once I reassured him and asked him to rebook any customers, he hung up; and I knew I would have a week to myself.

I needed time to think, to recover, to heal. Not just from my beating, but from her. All I could think of was Mia and the night we spent together. The feel of her body under my fingers, the heat of her lips on mine, how her hair tickled my shoulders, and her breath lingered hot and heavy on my skin. I was consumed by thoughts of Mia; she was just another beautiful thing I couldn't have.

I spent the weekend wallowing, mourning her loss, and letting her go. I etched every line and curve into memory; I noted each of her sounds, the way her body moved and danced against mine, storing away her smell and her very breath. She left pieces of herself everywhere and, like foreign souvenirs, I clung to them. For in time, I knew I would have to set them aside and allow them to collect dust as they rotted away in the recesses of my mind.

The weekend drifted away like a breeze, blowing through the workshop, and carrying away my self-pity and anger.

I wasn't expecting the banging on the iron door that rang through the workshop on Monday morning. The 'closed' sign was hung up, it should have been a deterrent. No one should be here. I ignored the banging, hoping it would stop.

It didn't.

I left my steaming coffee on the table and limped over to the door. I swung it open, irritation prickling my skin. The feeling fell away like autumn leaves when I saw Mia on the other side. Her fierce eyes, soaked in resentment, scanned my face and slid over my body. She took a step back, her mouth falling open.

"What happened to you?" her eyes flew across me, taking in my swollen face, my bruised torso and arms. The intensity of her gaze made my skin prickle, made me feel exposed in all the wrong ways. I should have worn a shirt.

"Nothing that concerns you. Why are you here?"

She scowled, "I came to get my last paycheque."

"Right, I've got it upstairs." I stared into her eyes, golden flakes trembling as she winced at my appearance.

"I didn't know you'd be closed. I…"

"Don't worry about it," I ran a hand over my face. "I fell down the stairs, just needed a couple of days to recover."

"Stairs?" she cocked her head as her eyes roamed the peppering of purple marks on my body.

"Stairs," I locked my jaw and ground my teeth, her look of concern burning my skin. "Come in, I'll get your money."

She followed me inside and let the door close behind her. Spots galloped towards her and jumped in greeting, his tail wagging wildly. "Hey buddy, I missed you. Did you miss me too?" Spots circled around her and jumped up again in answer. The smile that spread across her face was devastating. Pure, uncorrupted joy and adoration. I wished that I didn't see it, wished she didn't love him as much as I did.

She scratched his head and he wagged his tail, leaping on his hind legs.

"Spots." He turned his head to me, his body stilling. "I need to talk to Mia, go to your room," he studied me for another second and dropped back on all fours. He circled her once more and trotted away.

"Wait here, I'll go get your money." I turned to walk away, and she followed me further into the workshop.

"I have some other personal items up there I'd like to take with me."

I studied her face, then shrugged and limped away.

She caught up and cast a glare at my limp, "Are you okay, Gabriel?"

"I'll be fine. Like I said, it's not your concern." My voice clipped, my heart ricocheting in my chest, aching with all the things I couldn't say.

"Don't be like that." Her voice held a tinge of bitterness.

"Don't be like what?" I snapped.

"Gabriel!"

I limped away, pausing at the bottom of the stairs, glaring at the task ahead.

"Let me help you."

"I don't need your help. You've helped enough."

"What's that supposed to mean?"

"Nothing. Just come get your money so you can leave."

"Gabriel…"

I started up the stairs, each step shooting pain across my body. A peppering of sweat broke across my brow. I gritted my teeth and forced myself to put one foot in front of the other.

I pushed the office door open and stumbled inside. All of a sudden we were back in the room where she saw me, saw through me—raw and vulnerable—where she soothed me, relieving the anguish, and crushing my hopes.

I fought my stiff limbs and reached over to the drawer. I pulled out a pristine white envelope, it hovered between us.

She took it and placed it back on the table. "Let me have a look at you," her voice was soft and agonising. My core lit up with memories.

"Just go, Mia. Do us both a favour and leave."

"Why?"

"You know this thing between us can't work."

"Yes, it can." She leaned over the table and brushed an errant hair from my forehead, the heat of her fingertips singeing my skin with desire.

"You are not listening to what I'm saying to you." My voice raw, my throat dry.

"Maybe I don't want to listen." Her finger trailed my jaw and I winced. I was in all kinds of pain, and they all blurred into a single hot ball of raw, desperate need.

"Why the fuck are you so stubborn?"

"Because, we've got something Gabriel." Her eyes latched onto mine.

"No, we don't." I unglued my eyes from hers, swallowing the lie.

"Stop lying to yourself."

"Why are you persisting? All I've done is push you away."

"Because, I want to stay. Me and you, there *is* something. A current that runs between us, electricity—I know you feel it too."

"Mia, I can't...I'm just not strong enough." Something akin to fear settled across my skin.

"Not strong enough to love me?" her voice quivered, and all I wanted was to pull her into the dark void of my heart and fill myself with her, give her hope and comfort.

"Not strong enough...to lose you." Our eyes met and I knew I was lost. I pushed her hand away. "Anyway, it seems that you've moved on."

"What are you talking about?"

"I saw you with that man, on the swing." I spat out the words as they left a bitter taste in my mouth.

"Red?" Her eyes widened, "You were at the junk yard?"

My silence stretched across us, and I could almost hear all the pieces falling into place inside her mind.

"Red is a friend of my father's."

"He seemed *very* friendly." I sneered at her.

"It's not like that. I've known him all my life."

"Yeah, looked like you know him real well."

"It's not like that." She swatted the air with her arms and gave me a glassy stare.

I gruffed at her response and pushed the envelope back towards her, the sharp movement eliciting a wince from me.

Mia inhaled, the annoyance falling from her face as her eyes darted along mine, "It looks painful."

"I've had worse."

"Let me make it better. I can make everything better for you, Gabriel." The way she said my name sent a warm shiver down my spine that spilled inside me, making everything tighter, warmer, harder.

Tentatively, she reached out and touched my chest. "Does this hurt?" she brushed her fingers along a black bruise.

"Yes." I hissed at the touch.

She leaned in and kissed my injured skin. I flinched at the pain, at the pleasure.

"What about his one?" she kissed another.

"Yes." I bit my lip at the soft sting.

She kissed more of my bruises, sending heat radiating to my core. Her touch unravelling me, overpowering me, and tearing at my defences.

Her hands traced my damaged jaw, "What about here?" she touched another patch of tainted skin.

"Yes." I sucked in breath as Mia pushed on her tiptoes and trailed soft kisses along my jaw, her delicate touch unleashing desire, hot and deep.

"Mia…" I was breaking.

"And this?" she didn't wait for an answer planting a long, soft kiss on my eyelid. I shuddered at the angry pain and delicate pleasure.

"And this?" her voice was but a whisper as she leaned into me, her face a hairsbreadth away as she kissed my broken lip, sucking it into her mouth. I moaned at the tender, splendid agony. It was my undoing.

I wrapped my hands around her and pulled her to me, inhaling her sweet perfume as I kissed her, my tongue sweeping past her lips. Hunger and desire swirled between us as our mouths warred and tongues battled. Her taste stirred primal needs, stoking a fire I'd been trying to put out since she left.

I broke the kiss and held her as if she was about to break—knowing that she was the one keeping me from falling apart. "Mia, Luce mia. We can't, please. I can't lose you."

"You will never lose me," her lips brushed mine.

"Mia. Please." I stiffened around her, pulling my mouth away from hers.

Mia splayed her palms on my chest and tried to push away, her brows pinched, and her forehead furrowed.

"Let me go, Gabriel."

"I. Don't. Want. To." I choked on the words, even as my arms fell away from her.

Mia didn't move.

I didn't breathe.

"Tell me *why*. I need to understand," The golden specks danced in her shining eyes. I lowered my forehead so that it leaned against hers. "Tell me the truth, Gabriel." She whispered.

We stood on the precipice together—a long dark fall. I gave her the choice. I *needed* her to choose life, to take her money and enjoy a long, happy life. But I *wanted* her to choose me, to take my hand and plummet into the darkness, knowing that there would be no light at the end of the tunnel. We would always be falling, always be engulfed in darkness; but we would always, *always* be together.

Truth.

"Sit down." I could hear the tension in my voice. It was raw and crude, and I could barely swallow.

The truth will set us free…

PART IX

The ten days after Tony's death propelled me into manhood, I was birthed into a world that I knew lay beyond, yet I was not at all prepared for what I found on the other side. Like a newborn, I was often screaming, covered in blood, and not sleeping at all—weary and afraid of the vast, large world of beyond.

I was a newborn stag that needed to stand, walk, and run before the wolves got a scent of the fresh placenta still covering my body. But, as quick as I was, they had already gotten a sniff of my scent, and they snapped at my heels.

If I knew the value of the treasure I'd acquired, I would've torn through it on the same night I watched Tony die; and then I would have burned it. I unearthed a bomb and it was ticking in my hands. There were no wires to cut, or devices to disarm it. It was going to go off, and it was only a matter of time.

For a brief few days after the funeral, it seemed as if life had returned to normal and everyone fell into their usual routines. In the morning, the staff would show up, cars would be washed, and money would exchange hands; except I had no idea who was pocketing all this money or where it was going, and that scared me. I kept my head down, my mouth shut, and the books in order.

Tick, tock.

Three days after we put Tony in the ground Salvatore pushed the door to my office open, and Joe Romano stepped in behind him. I jumped out of my seat, the chair scraping the wooden floor.

"Young Gabriel," said the newcomer and stretched out a hand.

"Mr. Romano." I nodded at him, accepting his hand. We shook and he squeezed, just a little more than he had to—just a subtle reminder.

He flashed me a smile, a perfect row of teeth like a picket fence. "Joe." He pulled his hand away, and I gestured to the seat opposite my desk.

"Please sit."

He did—unceremoniously. Salvatore slid back into the shadows of the door.

"What can I do for you?"

"I believe you might have something that belongs to me." He didn't beat around the bush. His sharp wolfish eyes focused on my face.

"I'm not sure I understand what you mean."

Joe sucked in a long breath and snorted. Lacing his fingers together, he placed his hands over his right knee.

"Salvatore here tells me you've been running this place for a couple of years."

"Tony gave it to me after my graduation." I spat out the words. The memory of that night still stung. My fingers suddenly itched to soothe my back.

"And, I hear you've been a good dog,"

I sat back in my chair and folded my arms across my chest, hoping they would keep my heart from slamming through my rib cage. What did he know? What *did* I have? I didn't reply. I just waited for Joe to fill in his own silence.

"Dogs are loyal, yes?"

I waited. My mind drifting to Spots.

"You seem to be loyal," His face split into a grin that stretched too far across his face. "We all know what that filthy piece of shit, Tony, got up to in his spare time, and we all know how you kept your mouth shut."

I waited cringing inwardly. The space in my head filling with the screams. I remained silent, waiting for the wailing to fade. Joe shifted in his seat.

"I'm here to offer you a truce, Gabriel."

"Why do we need a truce? Are we at war?"

"No, we're all friends here—for now," he flashed me another smile and flicked light blonde hair away from his eyes. "See, it's come to our attention that you may have inherited Tony's collection."

"I have no idea what you're talking about."

"Indeed," he tipped his head a little, and the lock of hair fell back onto his forehead. "But, let's just say that you do—for shits and giggles." All traces of humour fell from his face. "Let's just say that we are prepared to offer you an out."

I looked into his green eyes, they narrowed glaring at me. He looked like a wolf that'd been bleached by the sun—smooth, and stealthy, and completely predatory.

Joe sighed and stood up. "I see."

He leaned over my desk with his palms splayed across the polished wood. He bore into my eyes, the warmth evaporating from his face. "Gabriel, this is a one time offer; a free pass, a way out. You could be your own man, do anything you want," he gestured with his hands around the room as if they drew invisible threads of dreams I could grasp onto. "In fact, there's a finder's fee, something to help you get a new start in life."

He pushed away from the table, "All I want is whatever you took from Tony's office, and I want it by the end of the week."

I ground my teeth, hoping my body didn't give me away. They knew. They fucking knew. Or, they thought they knew and were trying to smoke me out. Suddenly, I was the wolf and they were blowing too much smoke into my burrow. I sucked in a breath, trying not to choke.

"The only thing Tony gave me was this piece of shit place and that piece of shit man." I pointed at Salvatore who remained stoic.

"Indeed. One week, Gabriel."

With that, he turned away from me and left my office.

"You're playing with fire, boss."

"Well, maybe it's time to set everything alight."

Salvatore didn't reply as he stepped out of the office, trailing his new master.

⸻

Joe had managed to instil the paranoia beneath my skin. It burned deep and long, and I found myself looking over my shoulder more than I cared to admit. I teetered on the edge of self-destruction, I had no idea who I could trust and with what. So, I decide to keep all my secrets buried, all the skeletons in the closet.

The four days after Joe's visit had me sinking deeper into Tony's depravity and my own inhumanity; but, we'll get to all that. I need to skip ahead, to make you understand.

I was functioning on almost no sleep and deep seeded regret. In just four days, darkness clouded me and fear hooked into me. So, I wasn't expecting guests. I wasn't expecting anyone, especially not after hours. Well, not anyone that would knock anyway.

I grabbed my baseball bat and took tentative steps down the stairs, my knuckles white around the wood, and my heart slamming violently in my chest.

I peeked out of the small window into the night. My body tensed as adrenaline teemed inside.

"What do you want?" I exhaled trying to rid myself of the nervous energy inside.

"Nice to see you too. You going to let me in?"

"Are you alone?"

"Why wouldn't I be?"

I stepped closer to the door and peered out of the window, beyond the fringes of light. I searched the streets but couldn't see anyone else.

I unlocked the deadbolt and the door and held it open.

Rita slipped inside, an easy smile on her face.

"Paranoid much?"

"Something like that. What are you doing here?"

"Well, after seeing you at the funeral the other day, I thought we could catch up a bit." She gave me a heated look and took another step inside.

"Right, ok." I followed her deeper into the car wash, and she took in the silent machinery and darkness of the cavernous room.

"You live here now?"

I nodded, still trying to comprehend the purpose for Rita's visit.

"A step up for you from that other dump."

"Barely." I shrugged, dragging a hand over my face, fighting exhaustion.

"Well are you going to invite me in, or what?"

"Yeah, sure. Sorry." I ushered her upstairs, but, I couldn't help but keep looking behind me with each step.

"Geeze, Gabriel relax. It's just me."

I inhaled deeply, "I know, it's just been a long few days."

"With Tony?"

"Yeah…" I sighed.

"Yeah."

"Sorry for your loss, I know he was your uncle."

"Please, spare me. We both know he was a piece of shit. I bet you even the earthworms will keep away from that snake."

"Doubt it, with all that meat and sauce coursing through him. He would taste too good."

We both burst into laughter, and at last the tension seeped from my body.

"Would you like a drink?"

"Sure, what do you have?"

"Beer or whiskey."

"I'll have what you're having."

"Sure."

Rita sat on my bed and threw off her jacket. She wore a tube top that pushed up her breasts and showed off her hourglass figure. I couldn't help but look. Memories of the feel of her in my hands, the taste of her on my lips, flooded my brain. Heat rushed to my face and spread along my body. My cock twitched at the memory of her warmth. I clenched my jaw and turned to my small fridge. I pulled out two bottles of beer, twisted the caps off and handed one to Rita, who chinked my bottle with her own then took a long sip.

"Do you mind if I smoke?"

"No." I grabbed an empty bottle and handed it over to her. I sat beside her, the mattress shifting under my weight, drawing Rita closer to me.

"You dating anyone?" Rita asked as thick white smoke poured from her mouth.

"Dating is a strong word."

"Fucking?"

"Sometimes."

"Anyone special?"

"I'm not looking for anyone special. Or anyone for that matter."

Rita nudged me with a sharp elbow and took another long inhale from the cigarette, "One day you'll find someone that will fill your head and heart, and you'll be completely consumed by them."

I shrugged, "Is that how you feel with what's his name?"

"His name is Chris. And, well…no." She blew a series of smooth smoke rings, her full lips rounded in a perfect O.

"So, why are you with him?"

"It's convenient."

"For who?"

"Everyone. My dad, his dad, him, me." She dragged on her cigarette, the ember glowing orange.

"You?"

"Yes, me. I can come and go as I please, see who I want, fuck who I want, buy what I want; I just have to spread my legs for him every now and then. He's not even that bad in bed." She winked at me.

"So what about all that 'finding the one that consumes your thoughts' bullshit."

"It's not bullshit," she threw the cigarette into the empty bottle and it hissed as it touched the drops of liquid at the bottom. A trail of smoke rose from the bottle as she handed it to me. Our fingers grazed and Rita held my gaze, "The one I'm consumed with isn't available."

"So, make him available. It's you, Rita."

"Unfortunately for me, he'll never be available. Not to me, anyway." Her blue eyes pierced me with a sad look. I turned my head away, feeling like I should apologise.

I brought my beer bottle to my mouth and gulped at the cold drink, condensation peppering the green bottle, "Rita—"

"So, how long have you lived in this shithole?"

She turned the topic so suddenly I almost got whiplash. In truth, I was grateful.

Rita stayed for hours. We drank. We talked. We laughed. Her laughter made me feel light. The delight it carried as it rang around the cold room helped me forget—just for a short while. My tension fell away. The fear and dread that have been accompanying me for four days released their grip.

It was well into the small hours of the morning when she looked at the small bedside table clock.

"Oh shit, I better go." Rita pushed herself off the bed and curled into her jacket.

"It's late, you can stay."

"Thanks, Gabriel. But, I think I'd rather go." There was a hint of desperation there, or maybe a question that I should have answered. Maybe she just wanted me to ask again, or maybe she knew if she stayed that she'd only be hurt.

"Ok."

Looking back, I should have insisted. Everything would have been different had she stayed. Instead, I led the way downstairs and to the door.

"It was really good seeing you, Rita. It's nice to have a friend."

She wrapped her hands around my waist and pulled me close. I closed my arms around her and held her until she loosened her grip. She stood on her tip toes and landed a soft peck on my cheek.

"See you around, Gabriel."

"I hope so."

At that, she gave me one of her easy smiles and sashayed out into the darkness.

A nother day dragged by in slow motion. Rita left too early—too late—leaving me with little sleep. My mind settled into a fog. I had to keep control of the stewing thoughts that festered inside. The radio spewed out information about a high-profile murder of a judge and his wife. I locked myself in my office, silencing the world.

I must have passed out.

The shrill ring of the phone pierced the silence of my mind. I was sinking, anchored to a heavy weight that dragged me down and under. I fought the chains, gasping, screaming in the frozen water. My lungs burned and my body twitched as is fought. Sinking. Endlessly sinking. I bolted up in my office chair.

I was dry.

The world was solid.

My hands sliced through the air, reaching for the receiver.

"Hello."

"Gabriel." It was Salvatore. His sombre voice carried through the phone and hung heavy in the air around me. It wasn't his voice that sent the shiver to my spine, it was the use of my name. My heartbeat thundered and lurched, and suddenly I was fully awake, "What's happened."

"Get dressed. I'll come pick you up."

"Salvatore, what's happened? Is it Alice?"

"Get dressed. It's best you hear it from me."

"Salvatore, what are you talking about?"

"I'll be over in ten minutes." The line went dead.

I jerked from the chair and wiped the sheen of sweat covering my face. My heart pumped in my chest. I bolted upstairs to my room and found a clean shirt, then stuffed my legs into my jeans. By the time I was drying my face, Salvatore was knocking on the back door.

He had a key.

I had a deadbolt.

He pounded on the door, and I raced downstairs and slid the deadbolt open. I didn't remember locking the door; my head spun around, searching the darkness.

Salvatore didn't notice, "When did you install that?"

"Five minutes after Joe left my office."

His lips twitched, "Smart."

He looked me up and down. He looked haggard. Dark

purple bags hung under his turbulent eyes, and he looked like he hasn't slept in days. I guess having Joe around will do that—or maybe it was me, "Let's go."

"Where?"

"Something's happened."

"Does anyone suspect—"

He lifted his hand, silencing me.

"Just tell me."

"Get in the car."

The bleak darkness of the witching hour seemed to follow us into the car.

"Are you going to tell me what's going on?"

"I think it's best I show you."

My foot tapped and my jaw clenched the entire trip. My stomach coiled as thoughts and fear swirled in my head. Did we leave anything behind? Did anyone know? Salvatore sat stoic, his eyes firmly planted on the road. He wouldn't answer any of my questions.

It felt like the car was moving backwards instead of forwards. Wherever we were going seemed far and unreachable, the view on a loop.

I clutched the seat, wondering about Alice, wondering why I was surprised, and wondering what was so bad that Salvatore couldn't just spit it out. Were we running away?

We drove to the fringes of the city, where suburbia met poverty, where lines of humanity and garbage crossed. I knew places like these. I've lived in them with Alice. Cold steel travelled down my back and settled like a parasite in my mind.

Salvatore turned down a dirt lane. The tyres crunched on the gravel road, and angry steam rose from the ground.

In the distance, the black night was slashed by flickering red and blue lights painting the trees and hovering over the dry creek. Drought has plagued the city for almost three years; maybe the sky had run out of tears.

Salvatore slowed down and pulled the car over. We came to a complete stop, and suddenly I was glued to my seat. Either he had brought me here to leave me, or whatever was in the creek was going to be harrowing, and I didn't want to face it.

Salvatore stepped out of the car and opened my door.

"Come on, Gabriel. We only have a few minutes before the rest of the world swoops down here. Reg owes me a favour, it's the only reason I know, and he can't hold off forever."

I stepped out of the car, my legs feeling like jelly.

One of the police officers nodded to Salvatore; it must have been Reg. His hard eyes landed on me, and his mouth twisted in remorse. What the fuck was everyone hiding?

Salvatore nodded back and grabbed my arm over the elbow, leading me onwards into the darkness.

The dry creek bed crunched under our feet as we walked on, red and blue lights sweeping over us in a hypnotic rhythm.

And then, I saw it.

A shape at first.

Unclear.

Just a lump on the ground.

A vice gripped my heart, squeezing. Swallowing became impossible.

The light swept over the creek, and I saw her. Her limp body lying in a mangled heap.

I felt the breath leave my lungs. For an instant, I felt as if every muscle became slack, like my body was too heavy for my legs to hold, and the night stood still. Every sound became crisp, the air so heavy that I could feel it between my fingers.

"Rita," I gasped. And took a step toward her.

Salvatore held me back.

"You can't get any closer."

"Fuck you." I struggled against his hold.

Prying myself away from him, he blocked me with his body.

"Move out of my fucking way, Salvatore!" I didn't recognise the sound of my own voice; something feral and broken emanated from me.

"No."

"Move!" I shoved him. It was like pushing on a brick wall.

"You can't get any closer, Gabriel. You can't leave a mark on her, you can't move her, or touch her."

"Move!"

"Gabriel," he didn't raise his voice as I pushed against him. "Gabriel, stop." He sounded so damn calm as my insides felt shredded.

I stopped. My body stilled as the dust settled around my feet and my eyes fell on Rita's mashed body.

"Who did this?"

"I think you know."

I gritted my teeth at the vague answer. A loyal dog. A loyal dog who broke protocol and brought me here—or maybe he was told to bring me here. Even after the last few days, I found it hard to trust him.

There was too much to process, too much to take in.

I sucked in a breath and wrenched myself away from Salvatore. He stood back and allowed me a step closer to Rita.

Her naked body was broken and twisted, her face a frozen mask of agony. Blood trickled from her nose and along her forehead.

She suffered.

Because of me.

"I'm sorry," I whispered to the once beautiful girl. I took a long look at her, burning her image into my very soul, sewing it into the fabric of my being, and vowed to avenge her, to show no remorse. Then I turned and walked away.

Salvatore followed me out of the creek bed. A whispered conversation carried between two men, deep voices in the dark night. I trudged on along the path. All I could hear was crunching as the world flickered between blue and red, the pendulum of colour twisting around me as my stomach lurched and turned. It wanted release, it needed me to empty my feelings in a hot, steaming puddle of vomit. Instead, Salvatore's words rang in my ears. I pushed the feeling down and swept them under an invisible carpet, buried deep inside my emptiness.

I inhaled and rearranged my face, calming my emotions and trudged on. My heart throbbing. My chest aching.

Why?

But, I knew why.

White light swept the path and the hum of Salvatore's engine rolled along it. The car crept slowly along, following me.

"Get in the car." Salvatore's voice carried over the silence.

"Go fuck yourself."

"I know you're angry, Gabriel. But, more police are coming now—ones that don't owe me a thing. Playtime is over. And unless you want to get done for doing this, you better hop on in. If you want to finish what we started, this is your only chance. This invitation is going to expire in about ten seconds."

I stopped and looked up at the heavy tree canopy. It blocked out the moon and stars, or maybe it was the darkness that had fallen over me.

I stomped around the car and yanked the door open, slamming it as I got inside. Salvatore took off as soon as the door closed. Dust billowed in our wake.

The silence between us was charged, like I was a dangerous animal and he was aware that having me out of a cage was not a good idea.

"Why the fuck did you take me there?" I hissed at him through clenched teeth.

"I thought you'd want to say goodbye." He looked at me from the corner of his eye, and I could almost see a tinge of sadness.

My emotions felt raw; my senses frayed.

"Do you know who did this?"

His silence was answer enough.

"Did you know? Did you have anything to do with this?" My nails dug into my skin, my clenched fist tightening.

"No."

I wanted so badly to believe him. A flood of anger swept over me, "Why? Why did they do this? Retribution?"

"We covered our tracks. If they suspect, they have no proof—not yet anyway."

"So, why?" I dragged a hand over my face masking the prick of tears.

"You know why Gabriel. They want what you have."

My breath was charged as I expelled it from my body, "So why not just come and take it? Why the games?"

"Because, they thought she meant something to you. Because, they needed to send you a message, to make sure you understood what's at stake here."

"She's dating someone...was dating someone." I bit my lower lip thinking how everything about Rita would now be in past tense.

"That doesn't mean anything when she leaves your place in the early hours of the morning." He shot me a knowing look and his voice trailed, leaving a gaping hole of all that was unsaid between us.

"She was my friend."

Salvatore remained silent.

"Nothing more," I sagged into my seat, anger gushing through my veins.

"She's just an unfortunate casualty."

"A casualty?" I erupted, the nonchalance in his tone making me want to punch his face off.

"War has casualties.'

"This isn't a war."

"Wake the fuck up kid," for the first time his voice rose and his face took on a rosy colour. "By letting Tony die, you started a fucking war. By taking that money, by paying Crabb a little visit a few days ago, you pulled the trigger. Now, maybe you can end it all—one way or another."

I swallowed his words like stale bread, clenching my jaw, "All I need to break his code are the original files." It was a frustrated hiss.

Salvatore nodded, "You don't have much time left."

"I know," I raked a hand through my hair. "But, it's the only weapon we have."

"What you have, Gabriel, is a fucking nuclear bomb." He shot me a quick look that I didn't understand.

My body felt heavy. Too heavy. My mind clouded with a thick fog of agony.

"They were the ones that declared war, not me. They said I had a week—" My voice choked as I felt tears pooling in my eyes.

Salvatore cocked an eyebrow but chose to remain silent, instead looking into the horizon where dawn was breaking. The black sky forced away by the fringes of morning.

"If they want a war, I'll give them a fucking war." They were brave words from a scared kid; but, if you take me back to that moment, if I had to relive that night a thousand times, I would still make the same choice.

Salvatore's jaw clenched and his head tipped just slightly, as if he knew. "Well then, you need to prepare yourself for more pain Gabriel. Because more pain is going to come."

I swallowed hard and looked at the dawn of a new day, trying to calm my battering heart.

Three days had passed since Rita's death, and I had no time to grieve her loss—not in the way she deserved. There was too much else to do other than to feel. There was a weapon to build and discover, worlds to destroy and safety to seek.

My world kept getting battered by the force of the onslaught coming for me. I could lie and tell you I wasn't afraid, but I was scared shitless. I was twenty going on a hundred, and the last eighty years collapsed on me in a heap —now that I knew everything.

I'd been day dreaming again, playing with my own emotions, forcing myself to think about Rita, to glaze over her death as if it made me feel nothing. I had to dip my heart into concrete and allow it to harden, so that I could face all that came next.

Spots scratched at the door. It was past midnight, and I was so absorbed in my thoughts and trepidation that I'd completely forgotten to let him out for his walk.

"Sorry boy," I stroked his head and let him out of my room. Spots bolted downstairs and leapt against the back door.

I searched the empty street through the little window and unlocked the deadbolt. I opened the door a crack, and Spots dashed out into the night.

"Off you go buddy, I'm right behind you." I watched him sniff and piss along walls and knew the familiar path he took most nights.

I scanned the street again ensuring no one was lurking. I contemplated taking my bat, staring at it for a long time before deciding it would draw too much attention. I stepped outside and searched for Spots; he'd been swallowed by the dark.

I walked down the dimly lit road, paranoia holding my

hand while discomfort followed at the rear. The hair on my neck pricked up. Something was wrong, I could feel it right through me. The certainty flooded my body and shoved me forward. All of a sudden, I regretted leaving the bat at home.

I ran.

"Spots! Buddy, where are you?" I called for him, straining to hear anything over my ragged breath. I dragged air into my lungs and kept running.

Searching.

Calling.

The silent night was pierced by a bone-chilling yelp. The sound carried so much pain, it felt like a stab in my heart. It jolted me forward, adrenalin surging through me.

In the darkness, I could only hear his pain.

I got closer, his whining tormented.

As I approached, I thought I could make out two shapes. Running. I had no time to chase, as I saw the lump in the middle of the street. My heart pumped in my chest, hot blood crashed through my veins.

His face swung to me. In the streetlight I could see anguish in his glazed eyes as he tried to pull himself up, only to collapse with a whimper to the ground.

When I finally reached him, my heart crashed and guilt filled my body—drowning me, suffocating me.

"Hi buddy," I pushed through the debilitating guilt and reached for my friend. There would be time for feelings later. First, I had to fix this.

I stroked his head, and Spots let out a crushing howl then a wrenching whimper.

"It's ok, I'm here now." I looked around, the hair on the back of my neck standing. We weren't safe, we had to move.

I tucked my arms under his limp body and tugged. He growled and whimpered. His back leg, twisted into a mangled thing, hung limply as I pulled us both up, "I'm sorry buddy, we have to get out of here. Let's get you some help."

I resisted every urge to sprint, to run, to flee. Each of my movements shooting pain through Spots. The more he howled, the more helpless I felt, and the more the guilt tried to wedge itself back inside.

I pushed through the front door and placed Spots as gently as I could onto his bed. I ran to the door, slid the deadlock back into place, and grabbed my phone. I dialled the number, and he answered on the second ring.

"Boss."

"Someone hurt Spots. I need you to find a place I can take him."

"I'll call you back in five," The line went dead.

The phone rang, the shrill scream like the howls of a wounded animal, "I'm on my way, get him ready."

When Salvatore arrived, he helped me carry Spots into his idling car. Spots whimpered, his tongue lolling from his mouth, and his eyes rolling around in his head. I sat by him and stroked his face. I just needed him to know that he wasn't alone.

Salvatore navigated the car down narrow streets and around sharp corners, tyres squealing in the black night. My heart hung on the verge, a brittle thing about to snap. With each glide of the tyres, I had to fight the despair. I could feel my eyes brimming with tears, and my hands shook as I wiped them away. I felt raw, raw pain—raw guilt, raw everything. I couldn't stand the thought of losing him. My lips trembled as I whispered empty promises.

The sign was a large, yellow square that spilled its colour along the street like a beacon. A number of black paw prints ran across the sign and below the words "Paw Prints Rescue." Somehow, the name felt serendipitous.

Salvatore parked the car and tore a path to the front door, where he banged and pounded. My head throbbed and my jaw clenched; fear gripped my stomach and squeezed, everything was taking too long.

The door swung open and a woman popped out. She was dressed in what could have been her pyjamas, and her hair was pulled into a tight, white bun. As Salvatore spoke, she kept flicking glances towards the car.

He must have managed to convince her to follow him, because they both ran over with Salvatore leading the way, and the woman seeming uncertain. I can't say I blame her. If a man like Salvatore came knocking at my door in the early hours of the morning, I'd be reluctant to follow him into the street too.

The woman poked her head into the car, for a brief second her eyes fell on mine and then she noticed Spots. Her wariness evaporated and was replaced by deep empathy.

"Help me get him inside. Quickly!" Her rich, grave voice resonated in the darkness. Relief and gratefulness washed over me. Someone was going to help, somebody would fix this—him. This woman, with the empathetic green eyes, would look after my friend and fix all the mistakes I've made.

I scrambled out of the car and carried Spots inside, his agony weighing me down.

The woman walked ahead of us, turning on lights; they burst to life, waking other dogs with them. They were housed in large, open pens, two per pen in compartments along the wall. They howled and barked in a frenzy, as we stormed through the room and followed the woman down a dim corridor.

We walked into a white, sterile room with a steel table directly in the middle. "Put him down there," she pointed at the table and started switching on machines that bleeped and sparked to life. I took in the white walls and shiny tools; everything smelled clean, like it'd been bleached and washed down. It reminded me of Tony's back room, the place where terrible things used to happen.

My heart rate accelerated and thundered as she

approached Spots. She looked at him so tenderly my heart nearly split in two.

"And who do we have here?" She rubbed his head ever so gently, and her eyes examined him, scanning his body and coming to a rest on the mangled leg.

"Spots." My voice shook.

"Hi Spots, my name is Simone. I'm just going to have a look at you, ok?"

Spots whimpered and lay limp on her table, his energy dwindling.

"What happened to him?"

"I'm not sure," my voice quaked, the lump in my throat making it almost impossible to speak. "I found him in the street like that. I think I saw someone running away—"

At that, Salvatore's face shot up to mine but I ignored the look.

Simone reached for the leg and Spots snapped at her, his face curling with pain and anger.

"It's ok buddy," I whispered to him. "She's just here to help."

Simone gave a long, considered look. Maybe she realised just then how much I loved him, needed him, failed him.

"Ok boy, I won't touch it." She smiled at the dog and looked at the disformed leg as best she could.

"Can you help him?"

"I'll do my best, but I need some help. I need to call for an assistant."

"I can help."

"Can you administer drugs to a canine and operate an X ray machine?" She was calm but I could hear the irritation underneath.

"No." I looked down to my friend and kept patting his long body.

"Ok then, I'm going to call Alex."

"Does he need me to pick him up?" Salvatore volunteered.

"She and, no, I don't think so."

She reached for the phone and dialled. The conversation was hushed. Words like sorry and emergency drifted over to me as I held Spots, reassuring him.

She stepped away from the phone and rummaged in a drawer, the soft clinking of bottles echoed in the too-white room. When she approached again, her hand was behind her back. Salvatore's features hardened—his jaw locking, his shoulders squaring.

Simone's free hand came to rest on my shoulder, "I'm going to give him something for the pain now. I'm going to need your help to hold him down."

She stepped away from me and rounded the table, looking Spots in the eye, "Hey buddy, we're going to make you more comfortable now, ok?"

Her eyes flickered to mine and I pushed my weight against Spots' body, pinning him down as best I could while Simone administered the content of the syringe. Spots struggled a little, but his fight diminished even before it began. The pain had taken hold of him.

Simone walked away and I released him, rubbing his back, reassuring him.

Not for the last time that night, I was in a state of limbo. Salvatore leaned against the wall, watching Simone move about the room preparing utensils, pushing trays, and piling medication while I waited. I waited, listening to Spots' shallow breaths and scared whines. I felt helpless, useless, pathetic.

Footfalls echoed in the corridor, and Salvatore's hands shot to his belt. He held them there, at the ready, waiting for whatever to appeared at the door.

At the sight of the newcomer, his hands dropped to his sides. His eyes widened and nostrils flared as he watched her. Under any other circumstances, I might have had a similar reaction—but not that night.

"Hi, Alex."

"Hi, Simone." Her raven black hair was pulled tightly in a messy bun, and she was dressed in blue scrubs. Alex looked like she had just fallen out of bed, a sleepy, dazed look on her freshly washed face. Delicate, soft features attested to her youth, "Who do we have here?" She looked at Spots and froze as she saw his mangled leg.

"Meet Spots," Simone replied, the women ignoring us completely.

Alex cooed and crooned over Spots, then helped Simone with her final preparations for whatever procedure they were about to deliver.

"Ok, you need to wait outside now." Simone looked at Salvatore and then at me.

"I'm not going anywhere." I shot her a look that would flatten houses, and she glared at me, unfazed, as if she's seen it all before.

"Sir—"

"Gabriel."

"Gabriel," her voice softened and her green eyes pleaded with me, "I can't help him if you're here, and neither can you. We need a sterile, clean environment; every second you are here, you're increasing his chances of infection and of him going into shock. Please," she tipped her head slightly, "Let me help him."

A heavy hand landed on my shoulder, and I found Salvatore by my side. He waited. The room felt as if it was shrinking, the air oppressive. But I didn't want to leave.

"Please." Simone tried again.

Tears pooled in my eyes as I wrenched myself away from Spots. "I'll be right outside buddy."

My legs felt like lead as Salvatore led me to the door—which clicked shut behind us.

We stood in awkward silence as we waited. Alex's entry had stirred up the dogs, and the cacophony of sound drowned us. I was grateful for the noise. It meant I could stay in the silence of my thoughts. I knew Salvatore would have questions.

I only had one.

Would Spots survive?

I sucked in a deep breath, my chest heaving with the weight of the memory, pushing it away. I watched Mia, her wide eyes wet with unshed tears, the crease of her mouth, the furrow of her brow.

"Gabriel," her voice shook and vibrated through me, "You've endured so much."

"None of these things happened to me. Don't you see," I dragged my hands along my face, "They happened *because* of me."

"Gabriel…"

"Don't! Everything I touch turns to shit, and I can't—I won't—do that to you!"

"Spots is still here—"

"Barely."

"It's just a limp; Look at the rest of him, how you love him. I'd say he'd had much worse, and you saved him."

"I ruined him."

"You love him."

"I'll ruin you."

"I don't believe you."

"Mia, you have no idea what you're asking for. I carry too many secrets."

"You can share your burden with me."

"I won't put you in that kind of danger."

"Let me be your release."

"I don't want to hurt you."

"Let me set you free," at that she rose from her perch on

my desk and, in two swift steps, she was by the chair, her soft hands cupping my chin, "Gabriel, you are in so much pain. Let me make it better."

Her lips brushed mine, eliciting a low moan from my depths.

"Mia—"

Her lips sealed mine, my words dissolving, unspoken, as I tasted her; my hands finding the soft flesh of her neck. I could feel her pulse beneath my palm, her heart beat accelerated with each swipe of my tongue and squeeze of my fingers around her throat. Her skin flushed with fear and desire, with need and deprivation. It was beautiful and perverse, and I wanted it all—I wanted her. I sank my fingers into her skin, dragging them across her neck and into her hair. I wanted to punish her for not listening to me, for not leaving when she had the chance, for pushing and willing herself into my life. I had to be strong—for both of us.

I pulled her in ever closer, the feathery stroke of her tongue suddenly urgent, desperate. She purred at my touch, and my resolve almost melted.

Almost.

My fist curled around her hair, and I ripped my mouth away from hers. I held her there, just out of reach.

"Mia," my voice gravel, "Take your things and go." It was a ragged plea, wrenched from my throat.

I released her but she remained in place. Her clouded eyes clearing, as if seeing me for the first time. My heart twitched and twisted at the look of disbelief that crossed her face.

"Gabriel—"

"Mia, please. Don't make this harder than it has to be. I want you so badly, I'm prepared to burn down the entire world just to know you'll be safe. But I can't guarantee your safety—not to you, not to myself—and I won't have your death on my conscious. I won't have any part of you. Let me admire you from afar, let me long and desire you from beyond my barriers. Go. Find peace elsewhere. Make yourself a home."

I stood up, towering over Mia. Her lips a tight line, her chest heaving.

Without a word she snatched the envelope, rounded the desk, and rummaged through the drawer, picking at the contents, filling her bag with nothing but replaceable shit. She grabbed her stupid potted plant. The tall leaves loomed over her. Mia stopped at the door, her eyes lingered on mine —unmade promises broke behind them, unmade memories erased, all that could have been diminished in a whisper, "Goodbye, Gabriel."

I unlatched my eyes from hers and when I looked up again, she was gone. I watched her cross the workshop and yank the heavy door open. With a final glance at me, she stepped outside and out of my life.

At least, that's what I thought.

PART X

I woke up in the office chair, my already aching body protesting my movements. Stiff joints and heavy limbs resisted my attempts to reposition myself. I groaned as I shifted and twisted in the chair. I looked down at the desolate workshop. An empty shell. The thought like a blade in my chest.

A happy bark greeted me. "Hey buddy, have you been keeping me safe?" Spots jumped up at me wagging his tail. "Time to go for a walk?" He barked in answer and ran to the office door, running in crazed circles.

The day had faded leaving behind long shadows along the walls. Despite his enthusiasm, Spots walked by me as I hobbled down the stairs, he accompanied me to my room, and watched as I pissed and splashed water on my face. I wondered if he remembered me doing the same after his operation—following him into every room, supporting him through every action.

I shook the memory away and wobbled as I thought about Mia and her whispered goodbye. I sucked in a deep breath and headed for the front door. I needed to erase all thoughts of her.

I did the right thing.

I pulled at the door, holding it open for Spots. He leapt out, his mangled leg keeping up with the three healthy ones. He ran to a pile of dirt a few paces from the shop. Stopped, sniffed and barked at me.

"We're going this way, buddy, come on."

Spots sat and barked again. "This way buddy."

He ignored me and waited. I sighed and walked over to him, immediately recognising the pile. My heart slammed in my chest, and the world seemed to have slipped off its axis, making me feel off balance.

The potted plant lay shattered on the ground, the leaves lay limp, as roots protruded from the spilt earth.

Mia.

Sprinting back inside, my body forgot its aches as I reached for the phone. Spots paced around, his whines low and muted.

I called her number. It rang out. I tried again. It rang out a second time. I called Salvatore.

"Find her, now! Start with Stephano." I slammed the phone into the receiver, my heart convulsed in my chest as if my very soul was in cardiac arrest.

I stumbled against the table and caught myself, my legs unable to hold up my body weight. I stabilised myself and sucked in a deep breath, the air feeling too heavy, rolling down my throat like salty water. I coughed and spluttered and sucked another breath. Images of Rita's broken body saturated my mind. The twisted limbs, the broken skin, her terrified frozen eyes.

"No." It was a whisper that resounded across the universe, a promise to all the gods, a resolution. If they would just let me bring her back, I'd never let her go again. I wouldn't allow any more distance between us. I would protect her no matter the cost because, at last, I had to accept what I've known all along—she was mine.

I straightened my back and breathed in. The air slid into my lungs, filling them with purpose, with promise. I gripped the receiver and called Salvatore again, "Bring that asshole here. We have business."

"Be there in twenty, boss."

"You better be."

I hung up and went straight to the supply room. I grabbed a length of rope, letting the weight comfort me as the rough texture ground against my palm. I limped onto the workshop floor and found the remote for the electric hoist winch. It whirred as I positioned it near the middle of the room, then flung the rope over the hook.

A cold calm overtook me. I've been to war before and it had its casualties. Today it was going to be Stephano Fallo.

I heard the car screech to a halt outside and muffled shouting as the iron door swung open. Salvatore and Romeo pulled Stephano inside. He was kicking and fighting against them but, without his thugs to provide muscle, he was powerless.

"Bring him over here."

Salvatore and Romeo shoved Stephano forward until they could all see what I had prepared for him. At the sight of the rope, Stephano begun to scramble. He twisted and tried to wriggle out of the hold, but he was no match for the two men who had their hands clamped around his arms and shoulders.

With a shove, Salvatore and Romeo released Stephano, and he stumbled and fell in front of me. It was satisfying to look over him as he cowered on his knees. I had to remind myself that the purpose of being there was not to execute revenge—well, not entirely.

"Did you miss me, pretty boy?" He spat out.

"Something about your personality makes it hard to stay away."

"My personality is not nearly as pretty as your new face." He smirked.

My fists tightened by my side and I sniffed his fear, "Where's Mia?"

"Mia who?"

Nails dug into my palm as I tried to contain the savage anger that was building up inside of me, "Stop playing games, Stephano. Where the fuck is she?"

"Jesus, Gabriel, you're dumber than you look, or maybe I beat you so hard you just forgot," his weasel face contracted in a smile, "Let me refresh your memory; not five days ago, you came to visit me and my friends, and we had a friendly chat regarding Mia," his eyes shot up to the hook above his head, mine remained glued to his face, "We then proceeded to ask you very politely to stay away from her. If you need another reminder, just go look in the mirror." His smile stretched across his face.

I clenched my jaw and tipped my head to Salvatore who seized Stephano by the scruff of his shirt. In a swift motion, I grabbed the rope that had been dangling loosely above us and wrapped it three times around Stephano's neck. He grunted at the feel of the rough cord on his skin. I pulled the remaining length to his wrists and tied them firmly behind his back.

Salvatore released him.

He looked like a wild animal, captured and dangerous. Stephano leered at me—mocking—then leapt to his feet and began to run.

Romeo, Salvatore, and I remained where we were. Stephano managed five steps before the rope stopped his advances. He pulled against it, his face reddening, his eyes bulging from their sockets. He gasped for air and took a few steps backwards.

His head twisted back when he heard the whirring.

"Hey man. Gabriel," he took another step backwards, letting the slack in the rope hang. "Let's talk about this."

The hook continued to rise.

"Gabriel."

Rising.

"There's no need for this."

Higher.

"Gabriel, please."

Tighter.

His voice grew frantic as he tried to fight his restraints, but with every move he tangled himself further with the rope.

"It's better if you stop fighting," my voice remained calm. The sight of his petrified face goading me on.

The machine continued to whir until only Stephano's toes touched the ground. They scrapped, muted on the concrete as he gasped for air.

"Gabriel." He whispered.

I stepped closer to him—hung up like that made it easier to look into his eyes. "I kept my promise," I ignored his pleas, "But she came to me. She wanted her last paycheque—I guess she never got it."

I let the words hang for a moment while Stephano wobbled unbalanced, "She left my office a couple of hours ago, and now she seems to be gone."

I looked to his face, the red bloated skin instantly turning ashen.

"What do you know?"

"Nothing," he spluttered out too quickly.

I stood quietly and watched him struggle to breathe. His body dangling in a half-controlled fall.

"Gabriel," he choked and spluttered, "Let it go, you don't know who you're dealing with."

"What do you know? Who took her?"

"You might as well kill me. If I talk, I'm a dead man anyway."

I considered his words.

"Who?"

His feet scrapped the concrete, and his eyes bulged out as he lost his footing. His body dangled and twisted, fighting with the ground until his toes found purchase, and he managed to right himself. He gasped for air, the purplish tinge of his skin settling into an angry crimson.

"Don't do this." He rasped.

"Who?" I shouted, my patience wearing thin with his game.

"Rocco. Emilio Rocco."

I turned to Salvatore, and for a spilt second his face shifted. His brow creased and his mouth twisted. The expression was gone just as quickly as it had appeared.

I turned to Romeo, "Watch him."

I tipped my head to Salvatore. He made his way to the front door, and I followed.

Once we were outside, he turned to me, "You know the name?"

"No."

"It wasn't on the list."

"Are you sure?"

I shot him a look that erased any uncertainty.

"I thought we got everyone. I thought we go them all." The street light cast a shadow over his creased face.

"So did I."

Emilio Rocco. I would have to find out who this man was and why he decided to fuck with me and what was mine.

"Could we have missed anyone?" His stormy eyes grow dark.

"I don't know—let's go inside and find out."

Stephano was just as we had left him.

"Still hanging around, I see?"

He didn't respond. In the five minutes I had spent outside with Salvatore, he had turned a deeper shade of red. His neck hung heavily on the rope that was clearly digging into his skin. It was raw and angry and, if he survived this, would be extremely painful. The thought gave me pleasure.

"Who is he? What do you know of him?"

He took a shallow breath and lifted his head to me, "A relative."

"Shit man. Your family breeds like cockroaches, one in every dark hole."

"Well, this one crawled out from under the deepest, darkest fucking pit just to find you." His voice was raspy and mocking.

"Did you tell him about Mia?" My voice hissed, anger flooded my veins, and all I saw was a red-hot wall of pain that I wanted to unleash on this man.

Stephano didn't respond. For the first time that night, he didn't react at all. His silence was all the answer I needed.

"Where is she?"

"I don't..." he sucked in another shallow breath, "I don't know."

He was tiring fast. His body tensed, then fell with the effort only to tense again as it needed to remain upright to suck in air, to stay alive.

"Where?"

"Cut... me... down."

"Where?"

"I... don't... know," he struggled for breath, "Please." He begged. His chest falling and rising urgently with every desperate inhale.

I didn't want to be like this. I didn't want to be a monster, but this is what they made me, and I wasn't going to apologise for it. Fuck it, no one ever apologised to me. Monsters can't be weak. They can't show mercy, they can't allow cracks to form in their armour.

I turned to Salvatore and spoke in a low tone, "Find out what you can about this Emilio Rocco."

"Yes, boss."

With that, he stepped outside. A moment later a car engine roared to life and purred as it drove away.

I took a long lingering look at Stephano and tried to make sense of everything.

"Thanks for hanging around, Stephano," he looked into my eyes—hatred burned behind his weasel retinas, his chest heaved and fell with the effort of staying alive.

I turned to Romeo, "You know what to do."

He nodded in response, and I cut through the shop calling for Spots, "Time for your walk buddy."

"No," Stephano's slurred, strained voice carried across the concrete ocean between us. "You... can't... leave... me... like...this... Gabr—"

I didn't stay long enough to hear him beg.

⚜

We marched. Spots' leg dragged behind him. It dragged when he got too tired to hold it up. A pang of guilt shot through me. The streets were quiet. Everything felt *too* quiet—like the night I lost Rita. That night, her laughter and spirit were ripped out of this world so suddenly and violently that the world became more silent, more dim without her. Thing was, I never loved Rita. That scared me because it made me wonder what a world without Mia might feel like.

The walk was meant to clear my head of all the "what if's" but, with each step, the thoughts and images I wanted to leave behind haunted me, seeming to get closer instead of further away.

I turned back to the garage. Spots was getting tired. I walked inside to find Romeo and Stephano gone.

Who the fuck was Emilio Rocco?

As if the room read my mind, the office phone rang. I took the stairs two at a time, ignoring the shooting pain in my injured body. I yanked the receiver from the phone.

"Boss, there's not much. But, we did find an old farm."

"Where?"

Salvatore gave me the address. "Thanks."

"You need company?"

"No, I'll be all right."

"If you're sure."

"I am."

"And boss?"

"Yeah?"

"Be careful. It was one we burned down." I held the phone to my ear for a single breath and hung up.

Maybe it was stupid. Maybe I should have slept first, rested, collected my thoughts, and allowed my body to heal just one more night. But when it came to Mia, nothing was clear or clean or precise; it was muddled and messy, and I couldn't wait—not for one more second.

The drive blurred into whipping images. White and grey boxes, then green and blues with patches of yellow—a kaleidoscope of colour outside my black, agonised soul. My heart smashed in my chest, and I swallowed rock after rock as I closed in on my destination.

I turned onto the gravel path, the rocks crunched below my tyres, bumping into a mantra that hummed with the gushing of blood through my veins.

Just

Not

Like

Rita.

The road twisted like a sun baking snake. In the distance, I could see the structure—grey and ashen, as if it had exhaled and forgot to inhale once more.

I parked the car and killed the engine. I climbed out of my seat and holed up under a pile of rocks veiled by long grass. Everything seemed isolated. Empty. The long grass had been left to grow wild and out of control and had begun to recover the road. Tentacles of green wove their way into the cracked, dried earth. The unkempt field was peppered with yellow daffodils that seem to insert themselves anywhere loneliness grew.

I scanned the building. Once a barn, now a skeleton held up by nothing but memories and blackened, old brick walls. In place of windows, empty openings stood naked and exposed.

I lay there a while longer, my insides coiling and turning as if a fist had crawled its way inside me and was squeezing. Despite the urgency to run inside and break everything down, I had to be patient. I couldn't help anyone if I was dead. I scanned the area searching for movement. The place was silent, even the birds had deserted it.

I circled the perimeter, staying low, seeking out whatever —whoever—was waiting for me. But all I found was desolation and destruction. My heart sank.

I sucked in a galvanising breath and made my way to the building.

The door squealed like a dying rat as I pried it open. Light fell across the dark room, creating a long, odd shadow. Long charred beams rose idly in places where walls once stood. I waited, listening. I glued my back to the wall and crept inside. My heart strummed and my mind reeled. The place was deserted. That door made enough noise to alert anyone waiting for me. If someone wanted me dead, I already would have been.

I waited, allowing my eyes to adjust to the dim light. My

ears prickled with every creak of the rotten wood and twist of metal. This place was a death trap.

I crawled along the wall, staying buried in shadows. My shirt catching and dragging along the worn, prickly bricks; my shoes coated in dusty, grey powder.

I spotted a second door. The polished white wood stood out like a dove in a funeral of crows. The odd immaculateness of white against black forced all the hair on my body to tingle and prick up. I crept over to it, my fingers curled around the knob, and I steadied my breathing. Whatever lay behind that door would change my world forever. After, there would be no going back.

I turned the knob and pulled the door open.

My heart stopped.

PART XI

The first thing I saw were her eyes; they widened at the sight of me. The grip on my heart loosened and, for a moment, all the tension seeped from my body, and I sagged against the wall. My screaming heartbeat turned into a melody.

Alive.

I steadied myself against the wall and took her in. Her right eye enveloped in purple—swollen and angry. The golden flakes that usually danced, dulled, diminished. A green gag sealed her mouth, and I could see her nostrils flare, sucking air where her mouth could not. Mia's hair was plastered across her face and loose down her back. The light-blue singlet clung to her body, baring her shoulders and arms carved with red raw scratches.

My eyes trailed the length of the rope that bound her. It was a single length that bound her hands behind her back and her ankles just below them, stretching her limbs and restricting her movements.

I could hear her muffled scream behind the gag and see the pleading in her eyes as I stood and waited. She pulled on her hands, forcing her feet up. She pulled her feet back and her back arched in response, the rope chaffing her delicate soft skin. She looked like a frenzied, feral animal. Her wild, big eyes bulging as she squirmed and fought her restraints.

I waited.

It couldn't be that easy.

I inched into the room and stood with bated breath, my eyes never leaving Mia's face. I waited for movement, an attack, the flicker of fear in her eye, or the flaring of her nostrils. She was the bait and I was the great, white whale.

My body tightened, tensed and coiled. Nothing happened —and it was petrifying.

The dull, fearful expression on her face turned to hot anger. Her muffled sounds became louder, angrier. It was almost amusing. It was also completely intoxicating in all the twisted ways my body wanted it to be. The pulse of her heart throbbing in her elongated neck, the swells of her breasts through her tight singlet, her back arching as her legs spread.

I pushed the thoughts away and slid further into the room, my back firmly attached the brickwork. My eyes, finally wrenching themselves away from Mia, scanned the space. A hollow in the roof allowed just enough light to give the broken space a grey, dour look. I searched along the walls and began rounding the room, seeking any potential attacker.

I took my time, being careful. I listened and waited, shifted behind broken wood and burned out carcasses of furniture. When I found nothing, I finally detached myself from the wall and approached Mia. Her fight had dwindled, her chest rising and falling as she sucked urgent breaths from her nose.

The crisp, white envelope tucked into her waistline was as out of place as the door. It was too clean, too perfect against Mia's dishevelled clothing. I picked up the envelope and pulled out the letter.

'Do you see how it feels when someone takes something that belong to you? You know what I want. Consider yourself warned.'

I read the words over and over again, the chill spreading from the base of my skull along the length of my back, and soon it coated my entire body in a shell of trepidation. None of it made sense. Why take Mia and set her free so easily? What was this game they were playing at? The pieces were falling all around me, but I couldn't put any of them into place—too many jiggered edges that cut right through one another. My mind reeled.

Something was stirring. A monster. I couldn't see it yet, but I could feel it. It was coming for me, and I had to be ready.

Her screams pulled me from the paper, from my thoughts. Muffled and frustrated, she glared into my eyes. Her face red with effort.

Tentatively I grabbed the back of the rag and pulled it over her head discarding it on the floor. I reached for the fabric stuffed into her mouth and, as soon as I removed it, Mia gulped the air—mouthful after mouthful.

"You asshole." Her voice was gravely and scratched.

"I had to be sure there was no one else here."

"Untie me."

"Who took you?"

"Untie me."

"Did you see who took you?"

"Gabriel.'

"Did you see?"

"No," she huffed.

"Who did this to you?" My hand hovered just above her injured eye, resisting touching her.

"I don't know. The last thing I remember was leaving the shop; next thing, I have a headache and I'm tied up like an animal in this chair."

"You look like an animal." I couldn't help myself.

"Fuck you."

"I would like nothing more—right here, right now—to tear those clothes off your body and take you just as you are," Her eyes flashed with recognition. A primal, beastly need that she wanted to meet. "But you're hurt, and I'm going to take care of you first, then I'm going to make sure no one ever touches you again."

At that she stilled, sucking in a muted gasp, crimson flushed across her face.

With my promise, I made her mine and she knew it.

I bent down and drew out my knife. I pushed her knees apart—not because I needed to, but because I wanted to. The force jolted her hands and she arched her back, tossing her head back and letting out a pained whimper. I growled at the sight of her, bruised and broken and so fucking beautiful.

I sliced through the rope, her legs kicked out, and her body sagged in relief. My jaw clenched as I took in the bruised, chaffed skin and the deep marks left by the rope. I stood up, rounded the chair, and clasped her arm. I sliced through the constricting bondage. She moaned as I released her. The sound was somewhere between pain and pleasure, a desperate, ecstatic sound. It took all my will power not to take her just then, like the animal she was—filthy and angry, injured and tamed. I wanted to free her, not just from the restraints on her body.

I swallowed hard and offered her my hand. Mia glared at me. She looked fucking sensational, all angry and desperate.

She gave me her hand and I yanked her out of the chair, eliciting a soft cry from her. Her muscles would be aching and heavy from being hog tied, but I wanted her in my arms; I wanted to be around her, beside her, inside her. I wanted to be her world, to revolve around her forever like she was my universe.

I drew her into me and she tilted backwards, her legs

faltering. I lifted her and attached her body to mine, holding her in a tight embrace.

"Let go of me, you asshole. You left me all tied up like that for ages."

"If I let you go, you'll fall."

"Let. Go." Her bruised fists, battering against my chest, had no force.

"Don't be angry with me, luce mia. I just had to be sure we were alone. I can't save you if I'm dead."

"Save me? I don't need saving," she huffed and one of my eyebrows shot up.

"We all need saving sometimes."

"From what?" Her voice was suddenly unsure.

"From everything."

"And who's going to save me from you?"

"You should have saved yourself when you had the chance." We locked eyes and my lips longed to taste hers. I pulled her into me.

"Gabriel—" she moaned against my chest. I fought every urge primed into my DNA and pushed her gently away putting her down.

"Let's get out of here." She leaned into me, and her weight was a comfort. It seemed an odd thought to find comfort in her while I was the one who held her up.

She shuffled against me as I led her outside. We both squinted at the glaring sun that hung too high in the sky.

I helped her into the car and put the seat belt across her. My skin grazing hers as I leaned against her, the touch sending electricity across my body.

The drive home was charged. There were so many questions I wanted to ask, so many gaps I needed to fill, but I also had to take care of her—to soothe her, to balm her wounds.

⁓⁕⁓

I pulled up by the shop and led her inside. I lay her on my bed, where she stretched and uncurled her body.

"Don't move," I growled at her.

"I'm not going anywhere." She flayed me with a deafening look, and I had to force my legs to move.

I went to the bathroom and turned on the tap. The hot water spluttered and the shower filled with steam.

I returned to the bedroom to find her still on my bed. A fractured diamond. I went over, grabbed the hem of her shirt and tugged.

"What are you doing?"

"Getting you cleaned up."

She swallowed and allowed me to remove the sticky, dirty singlet stuck to her body. It peeled off like a second skin that didn't belong. Her body glistened with sweat and was decorated in grey ash, like a warrior after a battle.

One at a time, I stripped her from her clothing till she lay before me naked and breathtaking. My entire body hardened and screamed; my chest expanded with desire. I ignored it and removed my shirt. She watched me undress, her eyes hungry.

"You're all beat up."

"So are you." I reached out a hand and she took it.

I helped her into the shower and followed her inside. I grabbed the soap and poured some into my hands, working it over into a foam and started the delicate, agonising task of washing Mia. I massaged her neck and shoulders, the length of her back, her weary feet and long legs. Every inch of her. She moaned and the sounds made my hands heavy and my cock hard, pushing against my jeans, begging for release. Each touch of her skin was a delightful misery. I washed her long hair; streams of black ash ran down the drain.

I spun her around so that she faced me and pinned her to the wall. My soapy hands, breaking all the rules I had set for myself, breaching all the barriers, gliding around her curves. Her perky breasts responded to my touch. Her eyes grew with need as I moved along her shoulders. She whimpered as I soothed her swollen wrists, and she bit her lip as I washed between her legs.

"Gabriel," she moaned for me. My heart stammered at the sound, and my resolve begun to wash away like the bubbles in the drain.

Mia gripped my face and her eyes searched mine. Then she kissed me—a kiss full of desire and fire. We were tangled tongues and grasping hands; we were frenzied bodies and wild need. My swollen cock pressed against her belly through my jeans and, without warning, she undid my zip. Her fingers slid beyond the fabric and curled around my painful erection. Mia stroke up and down in rhythm to my answering hips, eliciting a desperate groan from me.

I grabbed her wrist, "Mia…No."

I wrenched myself away from her and growled at the pout she threw me.

"Let me take care of you first." She remained pouting but allowed me to rinse her off.

When we were done, I handed her a towel and peeled my wet jeans and tight boxers off my body. Her eyes flashed over my aching erection; I covered up, led her to the bed, where I lay her down and withdrew from her warmth.

"Gabriel."

"Don't move," it came out as a gruff bark. I retreated into the bathroom and returned with a soothing cream. I sat on the edge of the bed, my back to her pink, flushed abdomen and held out my hand, "Give me your wrist."

She moaned as I lathered the swollen, bruised skin with the cream. Her forehead creased and I wondered which she felt more—the pleasure or the pain. It's such a thin line that I don't think the distinction matters as long as I was the source of it, as long as I would be the only one to ever force that sound from her lips.

"What do you remember Mia?"

"Only what I said," she purred as I moved to her other wrist.

"There has to be more. What kind of car took you? Did you hear voices?"

"I don't know, it's all a blur."

I moved to her feet, and she whined as my fingers trailed the swollen path of coiled rope drawn perfectly into her skin, "It's a very long drive, Mia."

She snatched her foot away from me and sat up, her face crinkled in a scowl, "You don't believe me?"

"I'm just trying to figure this whole thing out, Mia. Someone is coming after me—after *you*," I wrenched my fingers through my hair and exhaled, "I told you, I'm not strong enough to lose you. I need you to help me piece this whole thing together."

At my words, she softened and traced her fingers along my bristled jaw, "I know. I'm sorry, I just don't remember."

I nodded and allowed her to settle back down. I took her foot once more and begun to rub the cream into her skin.

"Does the name Emilio Rocco mean anything to you?" Her entire body jolted. It wasn't more than a micro-movement, but I felt it as it reverberated through my hands.

She remained silent.

"Who is he?"

"A monster," She choked on the word and tears filled her eyes.

"Mia, do you know who he is?"

"All I know is that wherever he is, death follows; and I've brought him to your door."

"I met death a long time ago. Do you know where I can find him?"

Hot tears ran down her face, "I'm sorry."

"Mia, luce mia, don't cry. I'll never let anyone hurt you again," I wiped the tears from her cheeks, the heat scalding my aching skin.

I pulled away from her, my body already missing her heat. "You should get some sleep." I stood up and lifted the blanket, indicating she should roll beneath.

"You're not going to join me?" The hurt in her eyes tugged at my heart.

"I don't think that's a good idea." Her eyes burned into mine, her jaw clenched tight.

"But you said—"

"That I'll never let anything hurt you again, and that includes me. You are under my protection now, Mia. That doesn't mean we get to be more than this"

"Gabriel."

I forestalled her with a wave of my hand, "No! This is the way it has to be. Get some rest."

I tucked her under the blanket and fought every urge and desire to tear my towel away and take her like a savage, hungry animal. My aching cock twitched under the towel, and I threw it down reaching for dry boxers. I could feel her eyes on me but I couldn't turn back to meet her eyes. If I did, all my will power would crumble and all would be lost.

I sat on the chair facing the bed and locked eyes with Mia. She was so close and still the furthest away she'd ever been.

"Goodnight." I closed my eyes and wished for sleep.

⚓

A scratch at the door jerked me away from my dreams. In it, she was mine—and sweaty and naked. All my dirty, angry fantasies played out in slow motion, every pleasure lasting a life time.

He scratched again and whimpered. I sighed, standing up, my body stiff and sore. I opened the door for Spots who came hurtling into the room, his tongue hanging from his mouth. He leapt onto the bed and wagged his tail wildly. Mia squealed in delight and surprise, the sound resounding through my heart.

"Get down!" He jumped off and leapt onto me. "Ok, ok. We're going," he barked in response and ran to the door.

I turned to Mia apologetically, "I have to take him for a walk."

"Have fun. I'll see you when you get back."

"No, you won't. You're coming with us."

Mia looked at me as if I'd lost my mind.

"Get dressed, we're going."

"You go. I'm warm and sleepy." She pulled the sheet to her neck and curled her legs beneath.

"I'm not leaving you here, and I'm not letting Spots walk alone. Get dressed or I'll fling you over my shoulder and carry you bare-assed. Either way, from now on, you're going to be where I am."

"Gabriel, I'm not coming."

I ignored her pulling my t-shirt on.

"Gabriel, did you hear me?"

She tried again as I plunged my feet through running shorts and fished for socks in my drawer.

"Gabriel."

"You're running out of time Mia."

"I said…"

"Five." I pulled a sock on.

"Are you fucking…"

"Four." I pulled on the other.

"Gabriel, I said I wasn…"

"Three." I pushed my foot into my shoe.

"Fuck you…"

"Two." I was fully dressed. I stood up to my full height at the side of the bed.

"One."

I grabbed the sheet and yanked it off Mia. Her splendid, naked body taunted me; my own growing rigid at the sight. I went to reach for her when she squirmed and jumped out of my grasp.

"No! What are you doing?"

"I warned you." I made for her again, my hands wrapping around her waist and lifting her from the bed. I threw her over my shoulder, her bare ass exposed and delectable.

"Ok, ok, ok! Stop it! Put me down!" She huffed and tried to wriggle out of my grasp.

My hand rose, as if by itself, and the smack reverberated against the room, "Ow! What the hell, Gabriel?"

I put her down watching her rub away at the red hand-print on her ass. I smirked. Maybe, somewhere deep inside, the savage in me wanted to brand her, leave a mark, remind her who she belonged to. My skin prickled with the thought.

"I don't have anything to wear."

A smile crept on my lips, "I think you look perfect as you are."

Mia frowned, her hands landing on her hips. It should have made me laugh; instead, she floored me with the smouldering look of her exquisite body. I swallowed the rock in my throat and turned away, fighting the urge to take her, to claim her like a beast—savage and feral, and completely out of control.

Instead, I dug around in my closet for anything that would fit her. There wasn't much. I threw a t-shirt and shorts in her direction, both of which were too large.

"We'll have to go past your apartment later and pick up some clothes."

"And why is that?" She asked as she pulled on my over-sized shirt and tied the string of the shorts, which were completely hidden by the shirt. My body shivered knowing she had no underwear on, and one tug at the slim string would reveal all of her to me. My fingers itched for her.

I ran a hand over my face trying to calm the need. I cleared my throat, "I've already told you, you're going to be wherever I am, and I live here."

"Gabriel—"

"I can't protect you if you're not here. This is what you wanted. Accept it, it's final."

Mia grumbled something under her breath and made her way to the front door. I stopped her before she opened it, all my old instincts and fear rushing back. I went to the window and scoured the street, looking at every shadow, studying any unfamiliar shape. When I was satisfied, I opened the door. Spots looked to me, I nodded, and he leapt out into the street running ahead. Mia and I stepped into the road behind him.

"Tell me more about Spots, what happened after Simone fixed him?"

"I refused to leave his side. It took her two weeks but, when she saw I wasn't leaving, Simone made me a bed next to his. It was wonderful and terrible at the same time. For a while there, Simone was sure he was going to lose the leg. Those fuckers..." I couldn't finish the sentence. Despite the pain belonging in the past, it still felt raw—my failure.

"He knows you love him," she said, and I knew she could read me so well. My body constricted with the words.

"Love doesn't fix bones."

"It fixes enough."

She cupped my face in her hands, but I stepped away knowing if she looked at me like that, I would break. And maybe if she looked long enough and deep enough into my eyes, she would find everything I was hiding.

I pushed away from her, "If you don't stop touching me, I'll throw you over my shoulder and drag you back inside. You'll be guilty of wrecking all my good intentions."

"I didn't know you were capable of having any."

I bit my lower lip to stop myself from laughing, "That hurt."

Her lips curled in delight, and her eyes shone with menace, "Tell me about Simone." She laced her fingers into mine the sensation breathtaking and unfamiliar.

"Simone?" My mind drifted the to the night we first met; the judgement smeared on her face, the anger embedded in the creases of her forehead, the empathy reserved for Spots, the tenderness of her touch, "She's like the mother I never had."

"You have a mother."

"Alice?'

Mia shrugged.

"She may have pushed me into this world, but she's never been anything other than selfish."

"I'm sorry."

"Don't be," her hand squeezed mine. I inhaled deeply pulling away from grief, "Simone took me in, in the same way that I took Spots in. She took pity on me." I scoffed at the thought.

"I guess someone had to," She jibed.

"I guess I was just as much a mongrel as he was, just as lost."

I could feel the squeeze of Mia's hand as she reassured me and with a look, urged me to go on.

"I paced outside that operating room for two hours, maybe more. When Simone and Alex walked into the corridor, they both looked spent. Alex bypassed us and Salvatore ran after her like a dog in heat. Simone walked up to me, and it looked like she was ready to murder me. I almost smiled."

"Smiled?"

"It meant she cared. It meant she really cared."

Mia nodded, her hair tickling my arm, sending shivers across my body. I swallowed hard and continued.

"As soon as they were done, I asked to see him. She

warned me. She said he was heavily sedated and patched up. She told me to go home, and I told her to get fucked," I chuckled at the memory remembering Simone's angry glare melting into understanding.

"She led me past the operating room and into a recovery room. He looked so frail," My face pinched with the memory —limp and drugged on the bed they had prepared him, "I rushed to his side and asked Simone about his condition. She was tired and blunt; she said that she did what she could, but there was a chance he might lose his leg," I bit my lower lip at the memory and watched Spots as he bounded ahead, his bad leg tucked upwards.

"I slept on the floor with him that first week. I didn't leave his side at all. Turns out, it was good timing anyway..." my mind drifted away to those days. Maybe everything does happen for a reason.

"What do you mean by that?"

"Nothing that matters now," I clenched my fists at the thought and softened as I remembered Mia's hand in mine. "Simone took care of both of us. I paid her but I felt like it wasn't enough, nothing would ever be enough. The debt is too great."

"She knows how much you appreciate what she did."

I nodded, "Maybe."

We walked in silence for a short while, watching Spots piss on walls and sniff invisible messages left in a language only his nose could detect and decipher.

"Tell me about your family."

"Not much to say about ghosts."

I tightened my grip around her hand, knowing her pain, "Tell me what you remember."

"My sister killed herself, and I think she took most of my mother with her. She never truly recovered from Giorgia's death." Mia's body tightened against me, and her voice shook.

"Your dad?"

"He's been dead to me for years."

I didn't pursue the questions, I could see the pain as it fell across her features like a curtain of horrors.

"What about your farm? Tell me about it."

"My dad was a farmer, and I was the boy he never had. He had other plans for Giorgia. I wish every day that I could have taken her place. I would have done anything—" her voice fell away and her warm tears streaked down her face.

"Oh, Mia, I'm so sorry. I didn't mean to make you cry."

I winged my arms around her and pulled her close. Her body shook violently against me as she sniffed. I wiped the tears from her face, and she winced at my touch, her purple eye tender and angry.

"I will never let anyone hurt you like that again."

I pulled her to me and kissed the top of her head, wishing for more.

We walked back, each lost in our own memories—stuck in a past still too heavy to break away from, still pulling us down.

Maybe, if I wasn't so focused on protecting her, I would have remembered to protect myself. But she had me. We were entwined in each other's lives.

Glued together.

Inseparable.

I would never let her go.

Till I did.

M y body stung with pain; the chair dug into my back, branding me with a long stretch of pain.

I watched her sleep for a while, wishing I was lying next

to her, wishing she was curled up in my arms, wishing I was part of her universe.

I stood and stretched hovering over the bed. Even from here, I could smell her. Sweat and sleep had dulled the fresh soap of her shower and had made her completely irresistible, her skin almost copper in the early morning sun. She moaned and shifted. My body excited, needy—my mind overwhelmed. Her sheer presence tore down my defences. Her exposed, flushed skin unleashed desire so powerful I had to fight every cell in my body not to climb on top of her and bury myself deep inside.

I needed air, I needed distance. My body burned with longing so intense I thought I might crack at the seams.

I turned to leave.

"Don't go," she mumbled, half asleep. As I wrenched myself away from the bed, her eyes fluttered open.

"Sorry, I didn't mean to wake you."

"I don't mind." She turned onto her back, her hair a messy hive around her, her eyes half shut, her lips curved in a slight smile.

"How's your eye?"

"It hurts," she touched it tentatively with the tips of her fingers and winced, "But not as much as being apart from you."

I stilled and hovered over the bed. Something in her voice tugged at me, her hand shot out and reached for me.

"Are you ok, Mia?"

She nodded and her hand fell away.

"Gabriel, there's something—"

"There's always something," I cut her off. I didn't want to listen because I needed her so badly, I had to get away, "I need to work, there will be time later."

"But the shop's closed for another few days."

"I know," I pushed my hands through my hair, "Not that kind of work. I need to find out who Emilio is and what he's after. Just a few phone calls, and then we will go past your old place and grab your stuff."

"My old place? My stuff?"

"You don't live there anymore."

"Gabriel," she pulled the sheet over her body and sat up on the bed, "I'm not just going to move in here, I have a li—"

I closed the space between us in two long strides and pushed her back onto the bed, straddling and pinning her down. My fingers curled over her damaged wrists and squeezed. She whimpered under my touch; I tightened the grip.

"In case I have not made myself perfectly clear, let me do so now," my fingers clenched around the purple bruising, and I could feel her pull, trying to release herself from me. She wasn't getting the message, "From now on, you go where I go, you stay where I stay, and I know where you are at all times."

"You're not the boss of me." She struggled beneath me, her shimmering body making mine tenser and tighter.

"I think you'll find that I am. I own you now."

The sheet pulled away from her torso as she flailed against her outstretched arms, revealing her breasts. She moaned as I extended her limbs. Her back arched slightly off the bed and the sheet clung to her skin, folding around the protruding hip bone. She was the strawberry ice cream I never got to have and would never get to taste.

My body flushed under her challenging stare, and I resisted the urge to claim her as my own. The boundaries have been set. She would belong to me, but I would not touch her, I wouldn't taint her with my sins. I would protect her.

"The quicker you understand how this works, the easier it's going to be."

"*This* will never be easy." She bucked but I held her, my

grip tightening. She clenched her jaw, fighting the pain, fighting me.

I leaned my forehead to hers, sucking in her scent, and peering deep into the wonder of her eyes. Her heat radiated to me and all I could do was breathe her in. I slammed my eyes shut, fighting my body, fighting my desires. She was so close, I could almost taste her. Her body softened beneath me in an invitation almost too irresistible. I ground my teeth, wanting to grind against her instead, wanting to be inside her. This was too close, too dangerous. Her breathing became shallow, and I could feel her body heating, preparing, beckoning.

I released her and unwrenched myself from her, rolling away. "Get dressed, I have work to do."

"Did you find out anything?"

I kept my eyes on the road as I steered the car towards her apartment. "Nothing," I clenched my jaw, my grip tightened on the steering wheel.

My stomach rolled at the thought. Nothing. A vast emptiness. Something was stirring, a monster had awoken from a deep slumber, and it shook the world as it rose from the depths. I could see it in the markings on Mia's skin. I could feel the tremor of its presence as it stalked beneath the surface, shaking off dirt and ash, rising slowly to the surface. And it scared me because it was completely invisible—not a trace, not a single shred of evidence.

"I wish we could just run away, leave this behind, and go anywhere we wanted."

"There is no we, Mia."

She ignored my harsh tone, "But if there was…"

I played along, "If you could, where would you want to go?"

"An island, somewhere far and sunny."

"Sounds nice."

"Doesn't it?" She sighed and stared out the window. My stomach clenched at the sight of her.

"What if I told you, *you* could? I can set you free."

"You won't."

I gripped the steering wheel tighter. I wouldn't. I ran a hand over my face and played her game, "Ok, we could."

Her head snapped back around and her eyes grew wide, "How?"

"There's money…" I sucked in a long breath and questioned my sanity. I was trusting another human being with my secrets, a heavy burden I had carried for years. The lie was about to spill into the world and leave a trail. Once it was out of the box, there would be no putting it back. This would be forever, "Tony's money, I know where it is."

Her mouth fell open, and her eyes bulged. She sat for a moment, her hands slithering along her throat as she digested the words.

"Tony? The Hand?"

I nodded. She remained silent, absorbing. I sank into my seat, feeling lighter, "What do you know about him?" I shot her a quick glance as I pulled over, arriving at our destination.

"Nothing much, rumours. There was a funeral a few years ago, ten maybe—my dad went," Her voice trembled when she spoke, and I wondered what she wasn't telling me.

I killed the engine, and we sat in silence. I waited for more.

"Would it be enough to get us away from all this?"

"More than enough." This wasn't healthy, fantasies about a life we couldn't have.

"So, what's the problem?"

"Let's get inside, grab your stuff. We're too exposed out here."

Mia pulled out her keys and pushed them into the door. It opened at her touch, the keys left dangling in her hand, unused. I grabbed her as she made to step inside, her foot hovering over the threshold. I sidestepped her, gliding inside, and pushed her against the wall. I shielded her with my body and scanned the room.

It had been tossed. The couch had been ripped apart; cushions littered the small room. Broken glass and debris lay in disarray across the floor.

"Stay here," I whispered to her.

I took a few tentative steps inside, listening for any sounds. I was greeted with silence. My skin prickled. See, nothing is really silent, not when you're really listening. There are always small sounds; the tick of a clock, the hum of a machine, the breath of other humans—but not there. This place was full of nothing.

I sensed the movement before I saw it. I spun around to Mia, and the world slowed down. I called her name, and her eyes shot to mine, then swung to whatever was coming just over my shoulder. Horror painted her face. I swung out my arm as I spun, my elbow missing my unseen attacker. Whatever he hit me with did not miss. The brutal blow to my lower back splintered through my entire body. My knees buckled and I fell to the floor, gasping.

I turned to watch the assailant rush at Mia. He grabbed her by the throat and pinned her to the wall, his lips moving in her ear as her eyes bulged. Adrenaline surged into my body, and I jumped to my feet. My body would feel the pain later, now there was only Mia.

I reached for the man, my hand snaked around his neck, and I pulled him off Mia. His hands tore at mine, his sleeve pulling up and allowing me a glimpse of a tattoo on his wrist. Wings. Blue and green. They were not angelic, but rather a geometric design that was both rounded and full of edges. The image seemed familiar, and I tried to remember it. I could feel the memory forming, the fingers of my mind closing around it as the man bucked backwards. The back of his head connected with my face, missing my nose by mere inches. The blow forced my head backwards, and the radiating pain was back. I could feel the hot blood as it oozed from my healing lip. The split reopened. I didn't loosen my grip, instead tightening the noose of my hand around his neck. He gurgled and fought until his body went limp in my arms. I gripped his head, and all I had to do was twist. One violent, angry movement to crack his neck and end it.

But Mia was by my side. "Gabriel!" Her voice rang loud and sharp, "Are you ok?"

I threw the limp body on the floor and wiped my chin with the back of my hand, tasting metal, "Yes, I'm ok." I pushed Mia behind me and we made our way to her bedroom, "Stay close. They know we're here."

"They?"

"Come on out, I won't hurt you," I ignored Mia and called out into the room. I could hear him this time, or maybe it was my own ragged breaths and beating heart.

I took a few tentative steps into the room. I could see the shadow behind the door. Obviously, when they were handing out the intelligence quota he was standing at the wrong line. I edged around the door and, in a slick movement, grabbed the edge and slammed it into the body standing behind. I heard the "oomph" as the air left his lungs and repeated the action—slamming the door against him, again and again. He cried out and wedged himself out, rolling away along the wall. The man bolted up and, when he faced me at last, I could see the gleam of the knife as he slashed the air.

He lunged at me. I leapt out of the way, pushing Mia into the wall. My body tensed, all my muscles ready to attack, except instead of fighting, he ran. He ran past the couch, the debris and through the open door.

I turned to Mia, adrenaline slashing across my body in a torrent.

"Get your stuff, just the basics. We'll buy anything else you might need. Hurry."

I went back to the lounge. I needed to get information, I needed to remember that tattoo. When I rounded the couch, the man was gone.

"Fuck!" I slammed my fist against the door, the blow sent it slamming back into the wall, leaving a dent where the knob sank into the paintwork.

I came back into the room and watched as Mia tossed clothes into a suitcase. She emptied out drawers and stuffed them in. I followed her into the bathroom, watching her collect her toiletries. I allowed myself a moment to wash my face and rinse out my mouth. When I came back into the room, her bag was closed and she was piling books onto the bed.

"I said the basics."

"Those are the basics," She huffed at me. Her pout agonising and infuriating.

"Let's go."

She grabbed the books and headed to the door, leaving the suitcase to me. I noticed the pictures of Cookie and Jigsaw by her bed and grabbed them as I left the room.

I scanned the street before I allowed her back into the car. I pulled away, tyres screeching.

"Are you hurt?" Her hand landed on my thigh, the sensation of warmth making me forget my swelling face.

I pushed her hand away, I had to think, "What did he say?" My voice clipped and harsh.

"What?"

"I saw his lips move, what did he say?" I shot her a quick look.

She cleared her throat, "He said to tell you that Emilio won't stop looking."

I nodded a slew of thoughts whirling in my head, "Anything else?"

She shook her head, "What are they looking for?"

"The past."

"Why?"

"I don't know."

"Why now?"

I looked straight ahead pretending neither of us knew the answer to that question.

We drove the rest of the way in silence.

⁕

I winced as the frozen pea bag touched my face.

Mia's face crumbled, "I can't keep seeing you get hurt, I can't stand it." My lips twitched at her concern, and my stomach turned at her sadness. "It's all my fault. You tried to warn me—"

"It's too late now."

"What's too late?"

"You can't leave. They know you mean something to me now. If you go, they'll use you as a weapon against me."

"How? Who the hell is *they*?"

"Mia, I can't stand the thought of you being hurt." She rubbed at her wrists as I spoke, and my heart panged with guilt and agitation.

"Well then let's run away. You said you had money. His money..." her eyes grew wide. "Is that what they're after? Just give it to them. We can stay here with Spots and be poor and happy."

I cackled at the image she had conjured up. It was a sad hollow sound, knowing it would never happen.

"If it was that easy, I would have given it away years ago."

"So what are they after?"

"Something that doesn't exist anymore."

"What?"

"Mia," I took her hand in mine, "The less you know, the safer you are, *we* are." I squeezed her hand and her face fell, her lips pressed into a thin line.

"You don't trust me."

"I want to protect you."

"From what?"

"Mia—"

"No! You keep saying you want to protect me, but you keep secrets and I'm in the middle of something that I don't understand."

"Don't push me on this, Mia."

"Or else what?"

I tore my hand through my hair and ground my teeth. Or else what? I could tie her down and keep her here. Safe. With me. But to what end? I could force her to stay. But maybe she was right, and she had a right to know—at least a little bit. I decided on breadcrumbs; I would leave her some, but keep the loaf.

I threw the pea bag onto the table and gestured to the chair across from me, "Sit down."

"Not until you start talking."

My back fell against the wall, and I stared at the ceiling. An abandoned cobweb dangled from a corner and swayed in an invisible wind.

"Tony had millions in laundered cash hidden around town. It was in the walls of the buildings he owned," I could see her eyes flicker as she listened.

"He stole most of that money, skimmed it off the top, and

the people he stole it from were not happy. Not in the least. After he died, they came looking for it."

Mia dragged the chair around the table. The metal feet screaming against the cold concrete. She planted it directly in front of me and sat down. Her long legs crossed, her skirt riding up the length of her thigh.

"What happened to the money?"

I bit the back of my bottom lip and stared into her eyes. They burned with curiosity.

"I hid it. All of it."

"And you still have it?"

"Yes. Most of it…"

Her eyebrows knitted together, and I could see questions forming behind her eyes.

"Why did you never use it?"

"It wasn't safe and, by the time it was, the money had been in hiding for so long I couldn't just reintroduce it into the world."

"But it was clean?"

"Yes."

"But it's not anymore?"

I rubbed my hands along my thighs, "If I was to suddenly have a few million dollars lying around that I didn't have before, people would have asked questions."

"A *few* million?"

I chuckled as her eyes and mouth rounded in wonder. I've seen that look before; it was the look people get when they see an opportunity. It's one look before delight and another before greed.

"So where is it now?"

"Safe."

She rolled her eyes at my answer, "Stop avoiding the question, Gabriel."

"I've invested it."

I could see her mind ticking over, "So, we can use it? To get away?"

"We could, but I don't want to."

"But it's our future."

I cocked my head at her words. *Our future. Our. We. Us. Together.*

"Mia..."

"If we..."

"No! There is no us Mia. There will never be an us!" I growled at her, the words bitter and angry in my mouth, reeking of longing and regret.

Her eyes bore into me, anger flared behind the golden flakes, setting them alight, "Why not? It can be our ticket out of here." She sounded so convinced, so broken.

"Mia," I reached for her hand and covered it with my own. My eyes seeking hers, "I don't want more risk. More danger."

"But—"

"How can I make you see? Any future where we're together puts us both in danger. Can't you see that this is for the best?"

"This?" She snatched her hand away and waved it around pointing to the kitchen and shop that lay behind it, "Cowering in a mechanic shop? Hiding behind your cars and walls and excuses?"

"It's not cowering, it's being smart."

"You call it what you want."

Mia shot out of her chair; the force knocked it to the floor. She turned to leave the room. I reached for her hand, and she yanked it away and marched to the door.

"You don't know what you're asking for."

She ignored me and continued walking.

I grabbed her hand again, my heart pounding in my chest, anger flooding my veins, "It will mean war. Casualties." My eyes shot to Spot's empty bed.

"It's not a war. It's a fight for survival, it's a fight for our future."

She snatched her hand away from me as our voices rose. I stalked her as she rounded one of the cars, anger singeing the edges of my skin.

"You don't think I want that?"

"You just want to hide away in your room, like a scared little boy."

She walked backwards as my chest heaved with agitation. Who the fuck did she think she was?

"What the fuck did you call me?"

"A scared little boy," She bared her teeth at me, "You want to run and hide your whole life? Grow the fuck up, Gabriel."

Anger surged through me as I lunged at her.

Mia ran. I blocked her exit. The only way to get away from me was up.

She stumbled on the stairs as she ran. I roared and grabbed her foot. Her shoe came off in my hand, and I tossed it away. It clattered as it rolled. Mia shook me off, spun and kicked me in the chest. I stumbled backwards as she regained her balance, then tripped over.

"You want a war, Mia?" I reached for her again and snagged her leg, this time gripping her ankle in an ironclad hold. I yanked, my muscles aching at the movement. Her body slid and bumped against the stairs.

Mia screamed. A raw primal angry thing, her hair flung like a wildfire in the fields. She pushed me, clawing, digging into me with her sharp nails. I reached for her wrists, but she fought—a brutal savage fight.

I grabbed her wrists and wriggled my body onto hers, smothering her with the weight, driving her legs apart so I can settle against her, forcing her to calm down.

I pinned her down, my entire body pushing on her hips. One hand clasping her wrists, the other closing around her neck. Fury gripped me. It choked me in the same way I wanted to choke her.

"Is this what you want Mia?" I growled, "Violence? Anger?" My fingers squeezed the delicate flesh of her neck, she whimpered under the touch.

At the sound, I released her. My hands fell away and I lifted my body from hers. But before I could break contact, she stabbed her hands into my scalp and pulled me into her. Our lips smashed together, inflicting angry needy kisses on the other, our tongues tangled. Sweeping, darting, lashing.

I reached for her underwear and ripped them off as her hands found the button of my jeans and wrenched the zip open, releasing me. I didn't wait for an invitation. I thrust into her and she moaned as my hips thrust against hers. Her nails digging, scratching, clawing at my rigid muscles. My mouth entangled in hers with deep, bruising kisses.

I bucked my hips. Our bodies at war, at peace, pulling up, falling down; her fingers pulling at my hair, biting my swollen lip.

Our bodies collide in angry desire, tumbling down the stairs. I fisted a tuft of her hair and pulled as she screamed. Her hips ground and shoved, pushed and forced. Our chests heaved and blood pumped like a tidal wave in my veins, urging me, propelling me.

Pleasure.

Pain.

Up.

Down.

We were animals, ravaging one another with dark ferocity.

Raw.

Angry.

Ruthless.

I pounded, crazed and brutal. When she screamed, it was a battle cry, and when I growled, it was surrender.

She pulled my mouth to hers and sated me with a gentle, thankless kiss; then she pushed me off her and walked across the shop and towards my room.

"See? When you really want something, you fight for it."

She left me on the stairs breathless and dazed, my ass hanging out from below my jeans.

"Fuck!" I screamed into the deserted space. It should have never happened. She deserved so much better than that.

I pulled myself together and sat on the stairs, cupping my head in my palms. I guess I was going to war. I just hoped I was doing it for the right reasons.

PART XII

"Get up, we're going for a ride." I slept like shit and got up early. I took some delight in watching Mia sleep. She slept so deeply. Maybe she had a clean conscious. She rolled over and groaned.

"What time is it?"

"It's time to go to war. Now get the fuck up." I watched her sit up with a scowl then marched out of the room.

I sipped on my coffee. Salvatore would arrive soon, and we would go dig up a past that should stay buried. The phone rang. It felt loud in the suddenly too small room. I reached for it.

"Hey kiddo."

"Alice. What do you want?"

"Oh, don't be like that."

"Last time you were here, you nearly—"

"I know kiddo. Look, I didn't like it much either…" her words hung between us.

I sighed, "What do you want?" I had enough problems.

"I just wanted to say, I'll be scarce for a while."

"That's not unusual for you Alice, why the sudden call?"

There was a long silence on the other side of the line,

and I could hear the uncertain intake of breath, "I know I've disappointed you more than once, and maybe I'm not the mother you deserved, but you've turned out ok, you know?"

I remained silent. Something about "if you don't have anything nice to say and all."

"Anyway, I'm going to disappear for a while. After what's happened… I have this feeling something bad is about to happen. I'm going to try get sober again, maybe I'll get my old job back. I'll make you proud of me, kiddo."

"Good for you, Alice." What else was there to say? How many times had she already promised?

"Gabriel?"

"Yeah?"

"Just be careful."

I slammed my eyes shut, "Yeah, you too Alice."

The line went dead.

I was placing the receiver back when Mia walked in.

She had pulled her long hair into a messy bun, and her face carried the echoes of deep sleep. The bruising on her hands turned a sickly yellow-green to match my jaw. She rubbed her wrists as she grabbed a cup and poured herself a coffee.

"Where are we going?"

"You'll see."

She rolled her eyes at me and sipped her coffee. I smirked with the pleasure of making her wonder, making her want to know—making her want. My body purred with the unexpected pleasure of the thought.

"What are we waiting for?"

"Salvatore. He'll be here in a few minutes," we sipped our coffees in silence. Tension and uncertainty floated between us. How do we mend the gap we tore open the night before?

"Mia…"

My words cut off with the slamming of the heavy iron

door, followed by Salvatore's footfalls. He was at the kitchen door moments later.

"Morning Boss. Mia." He tipped his head towards her, and her face flushed. Her rosy cheeks tugged at my heart. "I've told you to stop calling me that," I griped at Salvatore who ignored me.

"Should we get going?"

I stood up and gestured for him to lead the way. I didn't miss the way his eyes flickered over Mia, appraising her slim figure. My fists clenched at my sides as we stepped outside and climbed into the car.

My stomach churned and twisted as Salvatore drove. The older parts of the city dissolved behind us as we entered the city's newest developed district. The whole place used to be an industrial area, a decaying part of the city that the government got tired of hiding. Instead, they decided to go with urban regeneration. They moved the homeless along and tore everything down.

Well almost everything…

It had been years since I had come here, not since we opened. The place made me nauseated. Despite the glamour and abundance we stuffed into every corner and plastered against every wall, all I saw was the blood the walls were painted by. The whole building was a monument built on death and made for profit.

As we got closer, I remembered the first time I saw the place. That day will forever scar my soul. Salvatore drove the truck that day. He seemed so calm, so unaffected by the events of the night before, while my insides screamed and twisted and burned.

The building used to be derelict. The grey, dull dirt clung on to walls like toddlers to their mothers, and everything smelt like piss. Now, it was a different kind of monster. I pushed away the memories as Salvatore pulled over and killed the engine. I held the car door open for Mia, who stepped out and looked at the building wide-eyed, scanning it up and down.

I watched Mia as she took in her new surroundings. She remained placid, calm. My eyes kept gravitating to her lips. She chewed on the bottom lip, and it glassed and glowed as it become more plump and pink with each pluck of her teeth. I shifted my weight, forcing my eyes away.

"What are we doing here?" Mia asked.

"We're starting a war, just like you wanted."

"I don't understand." She folded her arms across her chest and her face grimaced as a hot wind carried the whiff of morning sangrias.

"You will."

"When?"

"Now." I held out my hand and Mia hesitantly placed her palm in mine. I led her toward the door.

"Where are we going, Gabriel? I'm not dressed for this place…"

"You're dressed just fine." My eyes roamed her from top to bottom unashamedly, and my lips split into a smile.

"I can't. We can't just walk into—" she resisted, pulling against me.

I stopped and turned to her, her hand still clasped in mine, "You are dressed just fine. Because you are walking in with the owner of this establishment, no one will say a word, no one will so much as look at you."

Mia's mouth parted ever so slightly, and her eyebrows furrowed. She took a deep steadying breath, and her free-hand waved at the structure. "You own… The Hill Hotel?"

"I do."

She nodded, her eyes sparkled with anticipation, "How?"

"That's a story for another time," my mouth pinched together at the memories, "Now, will you come with me already?"

She nodded and allowed me to lead her inside, Salvatore following a few steps behind.

She was right, she wasn't dressed for this place. I had a sudden urge to throw everyone out just to see her cross that lobby bare-assed. The thought made my cock flicker. I ground my teeth, watching Mia take it all in. I could see her excitement as she took in all the extravagance, the opulence, the over indulgent spewing only money could buy. As far as I was concerned, she was still the most beautiful thing in that room.

The floor to ceiling windows ran the length of the lobby, and morning light danced across the black, marbled floor tigered with golden streaks. The oak reception desk was set along the back wall. Plush carpet kissed the marble floors in the modern sitting area to the left. Mia's presence turned a few heads. My skin prickled.

At the sight of us, the two receptionists stood up from behind the desk. I could see one thinking of approaching us, clearly appalled by Mia's dress sense, while the second raised a hand and whispered a quick word. The two straightened up, and their faces stretched in an unnatural smile.

"Sir, so good to see you again," the younger of the two women spoke, looking directly at Salvatore; a slow blush crept over her features.

Salvatore winked in response and her blush deepened.

"What can I do for you and your…friends?" Her eyes flashed over me, then swung to Mia.

At that, Salvatore's mouth cracked in a wide grin, no longer able to hide his amusement. The young receptionist looked confused at his reaction. She was in need of rescue, and it seemed that Salvatore was no knight in shining armour. I stepped in.

"I'll be having breakfast upstairs. Make sure the chef sends something up." At my words, her mouth fell open as understanding dawned.

"Oh sir, Mr. D'Angelo, I'm so sorry. I didn't recognise you…" she tumbled over her words.

"Don't worry about it."

"We didn't realise you would be here this early."

"It's ok." I made to leave.

"Sir?" Her voice was small as if all her confidence has been sucked away.

"What is it?"

The receptionist seemed to shrink and swallowed whatever she was going to say, "Enjoy your stay." She gave me a weak smile.

I nodded, "I want to eat breakfast upstairs in ten minutes."

I pulled Mia's hand yanking her away as the receptionist fumbled with the receiver, no doubt about to call the entire staff for duty.

"You're a charmer," Mia said as she followed me through the lobby and over to the entertainment areas.

We bypassed the dining room; it was packed full of guests all enjoying a meal from the extensive buffet. I may have gone overboard when I created the menu, but I never wanted anyone to be hungry when they left my establishment.

We walked on, the smell of croissants, eggs and bacon drifting through the space. My stomach grumbled.

At the end of the corridor stood a white door, I swiped my card on the card reader and pushed it as it beeped.

It opened up to a thin, private corridor.

"Still know the code?" Salvatore jibbed at me as we approached the private elevator shaft.

It only stopped on two floors, penthouse and ground, "Fuck off, why don't you? Go earn your pay."

"Sure thing boss," he chuckled and turned away, pushing through a second door.

"Where does that go?" Mia asked, her voice dipped in wonder.

"Sin."

"What's that?"

"The nightclub."

"There's a nightclub here?"

I nodded as I punched in the code for the elevator, the numbers forever scorched into my memory.

"What sort of club?"

"The kind of club where people pay cash for services rendered." She looked at me, letting my words sink in.

The elevator arrived. The doors pinged, flying open. We stepped inside and I pressed the penthouse button. The elevator shot up, the smooth ride took the usual ten seconds. The doors pinged and opened up into the hallway.

"After you."

I watched as she stepped into the apartment. My eyes swept over it, just to remember what it looked like; it'd been almost ten years since I'd last set foot in this place. It all came crashing down and I swung my gaze to Mia, letting her presence anchor me.

She surveyed the wide, airy living room. The curtains on the floor to ceiling windows had been drawn, allowing morning light to spill into the space. It kissed the opulent leather furniture and marble floors. It radiated off the plush carpets and ugly overpriced artwork. Her lips twitched as she took a few tentative steps into the room.

"You can go explore, if you want." I didn't know why she felt the need to wait for permission but, as the words left my mouth, she squealed like a young school girl and became unstuck, skipping around from room to room. When she was done, she came back to the living room and plummeted onto the black, leather couch.

I stood by the window watching the light dance across her delighted face. My stomach constricting at the sight of her.

"Do you like it?"

"I do," her eyes flashed.

I gave her a wry grin and turned back towards the window.

"Why didn't you tell me about this place before? Why don't you stay here?"

"Would you prefer that we do?"

"I mean… look at it," she waved her hand around the room, and it felt like it shrunk a hundred times over.

"I don't like it here."

"Why?"

Before I could answer, the staff elevator began to flash, indicating our food was about to arrive.

Within minutes the dining room had been set with a white table cloth and an overindulgence of food items; everything from eggs and bacon, to savoury and sweet tarts, an assortment of cereals, juice and coffee.

I thanked the service staff and once they left, I gestured for Mia to join me for breakfast.

"How many people are you expecting?"

"I don't like letting anyone be hungry."

At my tone, her smile fell away a little.

I watched her eat as I pushed the food around my plate, my appetite gone. I could sense the questions as they formed in her head, I knew what would be coming. I steeled myself for it, for her reactions.

For the end.

When she was done, I left the table and sank into the leather couch. Mia stood at the window, admiring the view from the fiftieth floor.

"Gabriel, why don't you like staying here?" I turned towards her, her eyes solemn as she studied my face.

I sipped the last of my coffee and looked at the bottom of the cup, knowing none of the answers were hidden there, "This place, it's a monument of my past life; it represents everything I want to forget. It's a place that's built on broken things."

I sucked in a long breath, "The garage, I know it's not much but it feels like home. It's where I can take something broken and ugly and fix it, bring it back to life with my hands." I shrugged. Maybe somewhere in my mind I felt that bringing machines back to life as atonement for the lives I've taken.

"I *need* to fix things," it came out as a whisper.

Mia was suddenly at my side. "Gabriel," she took my hand in hers, but I pulled it away. I was feeling too vulnerable, and touching her stirred too many things inside me. I would lose control, I would let myself have her. "Who's going to fix you?"

I pushed away but she slid closer again, breaking down my walls, exhausting my resolve. "How did you even get this place?"

"That's a long story Mia," I chewed my inner lip, considering my words, "This place is how I cleaned Tony's money. It's amazing what money and the right attitude can achieve. I tore down the old skeleton of the building that used to stand here, and I rebuilt. It's a beautiful thing, seeing something so broken come alive." My lip twitched with a melancholy smile.

"The worksite itself managed to launder almost a third of Tony's money. No one looked, no one cared. And if they did, all they would have found was Kevin Brown's shell company, which just so happened to manufacture and deliver building supplies and appliances. Just because a bill said a hundred and fifty air condition units were delivered, no one checked to see that only a hundred and twenty arrived, or two thirds of the carpeting or building supplies made it to the site," my heart rushed at the memory.

"Laundering was easy, and it paid off. Quickly. I watched the zeros accumulate in my bank account, and I built this place. I made it so that anyone that comes here would want for nothing. It's luxurious and exclusive."

"How exclusive?" She inched towards me.

"Exclusive enough that the likes of us shouldn't be allowed inside," I growled.

"The likes of us?"

"Filthy."

"As in rich?"

I shook my head, "As in right down dirty."

Her eyes flickered and her mouth parted. I scolded myself. I needed control, but being around her made me want to lose control, lose all my senses. I inhaled trying to regain my balance. "But like I've told you before, all that is behind me now. No more dirty deeds."

"None?" Mia's gaze pinned me and burned through me. Her hazel eyes hooded, her voice dripped honey and wickedness. Heat rushed through me and my entire body hardened, tightened, wanted.

I was undone. Without thinking, I allowed my hand to fall on her bare knee. Mia let out a sharp gasp as my fingers slithered along her soft flesh, stroking the skin up and down —small, measured movements. My fingers roamed the length of her thigh, finding refuge beneath the fabric of her skirt. They skimmed her cotton underwear where heat radiated. I slipped my fingers beyond the fabric barrier and her breath stalled. It was a beautiful thing; the crimson rushing to her face, the clenching of her thighs against me, the clamping of her hands against my wrist as her eyes widened and her wetness spilled from her.

She pulled at my wrists, but I ignored her silent struggle. My fingers roamed her softness, gliding over, around, beneath the one place I knew she needed me too. Her hands fell away from mine as her chest heaved, and her breath became shallow. Sweat erupted along her hairline, and she bit her lip while my fingers kept her on the edge—a delightful torture, a sweet torment. My fingers worshiped and swirled, swept and glided around her.

"Gabriel," she whispered, her breathy voice strangled and tortured. My entire body tightened at the sight of her. So needy. So desperate.

So.

Fucking.

Splendid.

She bit her lip, fighting the sensation while her hips began to move, seeking relief. I denied her again and again. She wanted dirty deeds, and I was going to play as dirty as could be. Her face creased with frustration, her body tensed with desperate aching. She looked wild and feral.

I pulled my hand away, and she moaned. Desperation and frustration leaked from her face as I sucked at my fingers, tasting her, needing her, aching for her. But we would both wait; we would both suffer. I should have never touched her.

I stood up and stepped away from the couch, admiring her, fighting the urge to finish what I started. It was almost too much, seeing her that way, "I have to work."

"You don't play fair," she scowled, her face fiery and furious, needy and desperate.

"Just dirty," I growled as I wrenched myself away from the room and into the office, slamming the door behind me.

I was agitated and needy, and was barely paying attention to my bank manager who prattled on and on, on the other end of the line. He was still talking when Mia burst into the room. She tripped over her words and fell silent as I held my hand up. Mia strolled over to the desk and sat on the edge, her legs slightly apart. My eyes zeroed at the apex of her legs. She had removed her underwear. Whatever resolve I had to stay away, to keep her safe, evaporated at the sight of the curly black hair and glistening lips.

I cleared my throat and asked the voice on the other end to repeat himself. I nodded, trying to concentrate on the words, trying to make sense of the strings of sentences coming through the receiver. Instead, I found myself rolling the chair over to Mia, my hands roaming the flesh of her thighs. Her scent calling to me, tormenting me. She was playing dirty, but I could play dirtier.

My hand slipped under her singlet, pushing up through the bra. I captured a nipple between my thumb and finger and rolled the hardening peak. She gasped at the touch. Her hips pushed towards me, and I ignored her. My fingers pinched and flicked the puckered tips, which swelled and tightened with each flick. She moaned and I coughed into the phone, covering the sound. Her face reddened and I flashed her a satisfied grin. She frowned at my game, shoving her hips closer to my face, the musky smell of her need overpowering.

"Thank you, I'll be waiting for your confirmation." I nodded at the phone and hung up.

My eyes shot to Mia, whose eyes burned with greedy need, "What are you doing, Mia?" I hissed and pulled her nipple, twisting the swollen bud, "I told you we can't be together."

"You can't just leave me like this."

"No?" My fingers pinched again, she shivered.

"Please Gabriel." Her husky voice whispered want and need.

"I like it when you call my name."

"Gabriel." She bit her lower lip, and my resolve collapsed to the floor. There was no more fighting, no more denial. I needed the comfort of her, the feel of her beneath my fingers. I stood up, unbuckled my belt, and released my erection from my boxers, sighing in relief. I grabbed a condom from my top drawer and rolled it on, and yanked Mia to the edge of the desk. I was acutely aware of her; her heat, her smell, her soft, wielding flesh, her searing breath and burning eyes.

I plunged into her, a gentle, lengthy stroke. Her body clenched around me. Mia caught her breath in a startled gasp of pleasure. The reaction shooting pleasure to my core. I repeated the action, indulging in her warmth, the narcotic pleasure of her moans and body. Moulding myself to her, above her, inside her. Her hips relentlessly moved against mine, her rhythm forcing mine. My restraint liquifying in the potency of her touch.

My hips pistoned and forced as she moaned into my chest. I pressed her body into my desk, not caring about the pens and papers and obstacles that pushed into her back, that forced her to twist and arch and buck. I clasped her hips and buried myself into her, pounding against her. She writhed and shivered beneath me, her rasping breath shattering as she violently splintered around me. Her body closed around mine, pulling, clutching, screaming. I slammed into her and fell into the void.

I collapsed above her, breathless. Sucking in her smell, kissing the moans from her lips, finding air in her lungs. "Mia..." I crumpled around her, "There are things I need to tell you," I plunged a finger into her hair and found her mouth. I kissed her deeply, hungrily—feeding on her, needing her, desperate. "And after I do, I don't know if you'll ever look at me like this again."

Mia wrapped her arms around me, and we rose from the table. She cradled my head in her palms and found my eyes, "No matter what it is..."

"Don't say it."

"Gabriel—" I cut her off with my lips crashing against hers. My hand pulled her in, my body ached with desire, with fear and with want. I released her and stood back admiring her quiet sensuality, her splendid beauty.

I pulled her off the desk, her long legs wrapped around my hips as I stumbled through the living area, and I walked us over to the bedroom. If this was the last time I would get to have her, I needed to do it right.

I lay her on the freshly made bed and kissed her jaw, grazing the slender column of her throat, kissing the hollow of her neck. She wriggled at the sensation as I rained kisses across her silky, scratched shoulders.

I rolled off her and, in one fluid motion, gripped her bruised wrists, pinning her hands above her head. She groaned at the touch, her body writhing against my hold. I didn't loosen my grip.

Her nipples danced and beckoned me. I taunted the pink buds, sucking them into my mouth. My tongue swirled and tasted as I licked and kissed and sucked and bit. With each swift flick of my tongue, her body quivered. My tongue provoking cries of agonised need that pierced though my skin, forcing me more rigid and engorged. I savoured her taste, spending time unravelling her sanity as she had unravelled mine.

I released her hands and made my way along her body, now salty from sweat and steeped in desire. I tasted every inch of her skin, grazing, savouring; taking a long, slow ride of culinary delight.

I devoured the long expanse of her legs, her meaty inner thighs, until I arrived at the apex of her legs. My tongue teased her lips apart and tormented the hidden morsel relishing in her slick heat. The need to torment her defied all reason. I punished her with leisurely lashes of my tongue, as it brushed and skimmed her wetness. Her low, incoherent mews ignited a hunger within me. Her white knuckles clutched at the sheet. I needed to gorge and feed and sate myself with her. Her breathing grew ragged, desperate pleas burned in her eyes.

She was ravishing.

I climbed above her.

Loomed over her.

My tongue skimmed her trembling lips.

"Gabriel." Her voice not entirely steady.

My heart strained at the torment etched across her face,

and I allowed myself to kiss her. Our lips fused and held, a long, liquid kiss that rushed lust and fire through my veins.

I broke away, flipped Mia onto her stomach, and pushed her knees in, forcing her exquisite ass into the air. My cock waited at her entrance. Her heat a maddening invitation, all my nerves stretched taut.

I waited.

Held.

Inhaled.

Anticipated.

Until...

At last, Mia pushed back against my cock, her hot, wet grip closing tightly around me. Reason tumbled into oblivion as I grabbed at her hips and pushed myself the rest of the way in. I wasn't gentle, I wasn't kind; but rough and savage, forcing all of myself into her. A desperate, keening sound escaped her as she threw her head back, and I knew she had lost her senses as I had lost mine. I plunged myself deeper, exalting in the spasms of her wet, silky heat, and with a final, brutal stroke, I unravelled.

We lay wasted, bathed in sweat and sex and lust—drenched in elation.

"I want you to be mine Mia," I whispered in her ear, the anguish leaching from my insides.

"I am yours."

I pushed away from her and stood at the edge of the bed, admiring her, noting every detail, taking her all in.

"I'll go clean up and then we need to talk." I grabbed my boxers as I turned towards the door.

"Gabriel..." she reached for me, but I took another step back.

"Tell me after." I gave her a dry, wistful smile and left the bedroom.

The coffee steamed between us, but I felt the chill in the air. It hovered around me, suffocating, waiting for me to fall, to stay down. The aloneness gripping its hooks into me, willing me to join it in the dark. I dismissed the feeling and looked to the light in Mia's face, the hope, my future.

I sucked in a galvanising breath, "I'm going to tell you everything. I should have told you before I put you in danger, before you became so vital to me." My eyes fell to the floor, "It would have been easier to let you go."

"I'm not going anywhere." She clutched to the sheet she had wrapped around herself.

I snickered, "That's because you don't know anything."

PART XIII

If I was smart, I would've left all of Tony's secrets piled up on his desk and let someone else pick up the burden of his sins. Fear would still be saturating the streets; puppet masters would be pulling the strings of those in power, and the truth would've been buried with the victims.

Maybe that's why I couldn't let it go. They were my redemption, my salvation. Although, I never felt that I deserved either.

I'd been agitated all day. Joe's appearance lolled me out of my comfort zone. Tony was dead and someone had to take his place, but that someone needed access to what they thought I had, and it was time for me to learn Tony's deepest, darkest secrets.

I waited until midnight. I must've checked that the car wash was locked at least three times. I checked every corner, every empty space for an intruder, made sure no one was hiding. The shadow over my shoulder kept growing, the paranoia gnawed at me.

I slunk upstairs to my room, locked the door, and pushed my bed over, sealing the entrance.

I pulled the closed curtains tighter and switched off all

the lights. In the darkness, I felt for the wall cavity I created. I pulled at the wood and exposed my treasure—Tony's collection of books and photographs, my get away money, and my grab bag.

I piled the books on the floor and resealed the hiding place. Once I had everything I needed, I grabbed the paperwork and sat on the bed. I switched the nightlight on and delved into Tony's possessions.

Some days I wish I didn't start with the pictures—or that I never opened that box—that I just handed everything over to Joe and wiped my hands clean of everything. But then I would've been just as bad as they were.

Except that I already was.

I kept my head down and mouth shut for years while Tony did this. I knew what he was doing. At least, I thought I did. And now that I could see it with my own eyes, I hated myself even more. He was a monster. But I was just as guilty for not putting a stop to it, for not saying something, or doing something.

Bile rose in my throat, but no amount of vomit would cleanse my soul. I hoped that fucker was burning.

After my violent induction to my new home at the garage, I lived in fear. I thought Salvatore was my friend, but he wasn't, not really. He worked for Tony. He didn't hesitate for one second to bend my arm and twist it behind my back. I bet if Tony had asked him to tear it out, he would have. So you have to understand, I was a kid. A hungry kid. And warmth trumped bravery, a roof over my head trumped justice, and food…that trumped my humanity.

I thumbed through the pictures, Tony's voice pierced my mind and the snap of the belt on my skin echoed around my head, "Mouth shut, head down."

I clenched my jaw, my knuckles whitened as I gripped the photo, forcing myself to look. To bear witness, to be held accountable.

Tony was a twisted, cruel motherfucker. He was a rat and he pulled everyone into the sewer with him.

He was a resourceful man. He kept his ear to the ground and when he got a whiff of nefarious activity, he sent his hounds sniffing—collecting, entrapping.

Tony listened. He listened to everything that wasn't being said. Like when the men around him joked about their wives, how tight they were, how old and used. He pried some more until they confessed their desire to fuck a young blonde, half their age; or when they beat up gay men on the street, he would watch the faces, the eyes as those men cringed internally. He would feed them with drink till they confessed their need to suck a cock; or when he saw the flash of delight in their eyes when they bound, or maimed, or humiliated. He dug into their soul until they spilt their craving to be gagged and lashed. Their secrets were his and they grew in their demands.

Tony was their fucking fairy godmother. They wished and he made their twisted commands come to life. The more Tony provided, the more they needed, the more brutal they became, the more perverse and cruel.

These men. They were not your everyday joes. They were men of power and influence. They were judges and politicians, peace makers and influencers, and Tony had each and every one of them by the balls.

Tony set up their fantasies and recorded each and every one—very scream, every grunt, every horror—and with each tape, he became stronger, more influential, more powerful.

Tony used those recordings for his benefit. Blackmail. Protection. Control. He turned the city in one large blindspot. He became untouchable. Which is why I never understood why I was hounded after his death, when I should have been given a fucking medal.

I slayed the king.

But 'The Hand'—that twisted bastard—power wasn't enough for him, not without total control.

Tony didn't do anything for free. His insidious nature demanded that he held the upper hand, controlled, twisted, and ruled.

Tony's business ran on supply and demand. But not just his own, the demand of others. See, Tony wasn't the only bastard around. Plenty of criminals need protection, a helping hand, a shield of sorts, and Tony was prepared to take anyone under his wing as long as they were prepared to pay the price.

Turns out money blackens the souls of greedy men, and they were prepared to pay, were prepared to smear their stains on the backs of the innocent.

Tony took his payment like the greedy pig he was. Payment for which I was a silent witness. I didn't see. I just heard. The pleading. The screaming. The muted sobs. When I bought the garage, I tore them from the walls. They were raked with guilt and anger.

These men paid in blood; not their own of course, but that of children. The innocent, first blood that should be reserved for lovers and teenage experimentation. Tony took from them the only precious thing they had—children. Girls, boys…Tony didn't have a preference, as long as they were available as payment for his silence and help whenever he asked.

I sat in a pool of polaroids.

Naked, bound skin, exposed flesh and harried faces frozen in terror. Their frightened, fearful eyes all looked into mine in paralysed frozen stares. All asking the same question, why didn't you come? Why didn't you help? Why didn't you stop him?

Head down mouth shut.

I swept my hands along my face and brushed away the hot tears as they slid down my face. I didn't cry for myself, I didn't deserve any tears. I let all this happen. I cried for them, the horror they must have endured, the payment for the sins of their fathers. I understood then, why all those men came to his funeral. They all wanted to make sure he was dead. No one cared for Tony. They just wanted their children safe and their conscious cleared.

I flipped the pictures over and noted the initials and numbers jotted in neat blue pen at the top right of each picture.

I scrambled off my bed, grappling with the pictures, stuffing them back into the box. Their existence burned a hole in my soul.

My breath came in shallow, ragged drags and pushed away the horror. It would have to wait. There was more work to be done, more to uncover.

I grabbed the first of the books and flipped it open. The faded green cover marked with a fatty hand print, the last trace of Tony.

As soon as I scanned the first page, I knew it was what Joe was after. I wondered what *his* crime was.

The book was divided into columns. In the first, initials. Two letters in rounded blue ink. In the next, a series of letters. Various combinations I couldn't work out. With no obvious patterns or answers, I moved on to the third column. Each line had a series of numbers. In the same way I had studied the letters, I tried to decipher the numbers searching for patterns. Searching for the obvious first; dates, bank accounts, longitude and latitude. As I ran theories through my mind, they each fell down like dominoes. I looked at the meticulous hand writing, wishing it would explain itself. Frustrated I slammed the book shut and moved on to the next.

The last book was a poorly disguised book for Tony's money laundering. Amounts and totals added up to millions.

Tony was stealing everywhere, and I needed to get to that money before anyone else would.

I paced in my room, feeling like a trapped animal. The walls closed in and if I didn't find answers they would squash me. I needed help, I needed an ally, I needed someone I could trust. A loyal soldier. A good dog.

My heart slammed in my chest as I dialled his number. It was a gamble, but one I had to take. I forced the air from my lungs as the line rang.

"What did Tony have on you?"

"You don't know yet?" Salvatore didn't sound surprised.

"So he had something?"

"Why else would I have worked for that piece of shit for so long?"

I took a moment to think about his words, "Who do you work for now?"

The silence stretched between us, tight and tense.

"Tell me what you did, and I'll find a way to release you. I just need your help."

More silence.

"You can trust me."

"But can you trust me?" I heard the edge in his voice.

Could I?

"I don't want to force your loyalty."

He snickered on the other side of the line, "Then what the hell do you want?"

Now or never. Leap or walk away, "I want you to help me dig up Tony's money and hide it."

I waited, the cords of my neck pulling taut as I waited for his answer. I could hear the blood as it rushed around my body, my heart chugging. I had just placed my life in his hands. Salvatore may never be my friend, but he could be a partner.

"What do you need?"

My entire body deflated at his words, the tension leeching out.

"Tools. We need to break some walls. And a truck. And a place to hide everything."

"Is that all?" I could hear the sarcasm as it spilt from his lips.

"Can you get it done?"

"Tomorrow night." The line went dead and my heart slammed in my chest. Could I trust Salvatore?

Only time would tell.

I packed away Tony's possessions. The need to wash myself, cleanse myself of him, strong and desperate. Instead I reached for a beer, I gulped down the cold beverage and mulled over the letters and numbers in my head, trying to decipher their meaning. In the meantime, I had to survive another day.

The walls fell away and dust swirled in the air like snow. The wall crumbled beneath the brute strength of the crowbar. My muscles ached and screamed with the effort. It had been a long night, and we still had the entire pizza shop to strip.

Salvatore looked as if he had been in a blizzard. His jet-black hair covered in white plaster particles that coated his face and clothes. They attached themselves to every surface and orifice. I suspected I looked much the same.

The plaster board fell away with a thud, and the room filled with a puff of white particles. Salvatore and I got to work.

The money had been stored in vacuum packed bags, just like in all the other hiding places. Being so well packed made them easy to remove. In the darkness, we loaded the bricks into the back of the waiting trolley and wheeled them outside to the waiting truck. It was already mostly filled with the rest of the loot. We knew we only had one night to make this money disappear. We pushed ourselves beyond our physical limits to get it done. This was the last stop.

We got in and drove in silence, the headlights slicing the dark road.

The car slowed as we approached a derelict building in the industrial part of the city. Salvatore pulled up to the curb, the engine idled as we sat there. I'm not sure what I was waiting for, but then Salvatore exhaled a long, resigned breath and started to talk.

"I was just a kid, like you. I was seventeen. We went to a party, things got out of hand. A fight broke out, punches were thrown," his breathing became faster as if he was back there, reliving the nightmare, "It was just an accident, but there was a fucking security camera that recorded the whole thing, and then there was the dead kid…"

Remorse and anger filled his voice, his knuckles whitened against the steering wheel, "It was just a fucking accident."

He brushed his face with his hands and for a second he didn't look like a man in his thirties, but an old, haunted man that's lived hundreds of lifetimes.

"Tony stepped in to *help*," he scoffed and shrugged as if the rest was self-explanatory.

I don't know why he talked, maybe it was the endless silence, maybe his body was in so much physical pain, it let down the barriers inside his mind.

I remained silent, letting him sink into his own guilt. Thing was, I didn't have to say anything. We had both just put our lives in each other's laps, and it was up to us to cradle the other if we were going to come out unscathed on the other side.

The building was a shell of what it may have been in another lifetime. Grime and dirt clung to the concrete walls that reeked of piss and vomit, and were decorated with crud graffiti.

"How did you find this place?"

"Tony used it."

"For what?"

"Do you really want to know?

I shook my head, fine powder falling from me like fresh snow, "Who's is it?"

"This building belongs to Judge George Crabb."

The name rang a bell in the back of my mind. A fine line of text flashed in the back of my mind.

Hon GC

ML. P. PTA.

548548747

I searched the recesses of my mind, wondering what those letters could mean. Just like before it came up empty.

"What are we doing here?"

"We're going to hide the money here, and tomorrow you are going to get the judge to sign this building over to you."

I stood there with my mouth falling open, "How do you expect me to get him to do that?"

"Blackmail."

I stared at Salvatore, who was already loading money onto the trolley. My brain as tired as the rest of my body, "I haven't figured everything out yet, I don't have anything on him."

"He doesn't need to know that," Salvatore shrugged and threw another stack of bills onto the trolley.

"If I go to him, I'll confirm that I have what they want."

Salvatore dropped the brick of money and straightened up. He looked at me, his face tired and drawn, "They know what you have. They're playing games, buying themselves time, giving you a chance to make it easier on everyone." He shrugged, "You've already poured gasoline everywhere, you might as well flick that match."

We worked in silence, offloading the money from the truck and piling it up in the basement. Salvatore installed a lock on the door, and we drove away into the breaking dawn.

⁓⊕⁓

I barely slept.

The scalding shower washed away plaster, paint and my dirty deeds. I looked haggard, my face drawn and hair limp. I was already feeling the lack of sleep and food catch up with me, but there was too much work to do.

Salvatore was immaculate. Dressed in his black suit and a crisp, white button-up shirt. He looked me up and down when I opened the door. I wore my best cheap suit. He scratched his chin as he appraised me, "Ready?"

I nodded solemnly, scrapping a hand through my hair, unsure if I would ever be ready for what needed to be done. I knew I wasn't prepared. I wasn't ready. But I was out of time.

Tick, tock.

My knee bounced up and down as we drove. The jumping limb incapable of hiding the tension I held. The silence gnawed at me, clamping its hands around my throat. When we finally parked, I had a lump the size of my fist in my throat, and I struggled to swallow it down.

"Are you sure this is the way it has to be done?"

"That depends, do you want to live?"

I sighed and pushed against the car door, forcing it open, "Ok, let's go."

Even though we parked down the street, we closed the doors with a muted thud. We needed the element of surprise, or we were fucked. I would be fucked. Salvatore might still have had a way out, and I wasn't entirely sure how quickly he would be willing to throw me under the bus if it all went wrong.

We walked the short distance in silence, the air buzzing around me.

The house was a two-storey colonial building. White walls and a perfectly manicured lawn. It was all too perfect, a facade to hide the savagery that lay beyond the walls.

A single car was parked in the driveway. Salvatore and I exchanged a look and walked up to the front door.

Salvatore used his elbow to ring the doorbell. It chimed heavily in the house.

A moment later the door swung open, and a petite woman appeared. She was unremarkable in every way, the only memorable feature was her too-bright red hair that came out of a bottle and stained the skin around her forehead.

"Can I help you?" Her feline eyes assessed my face, then shot over to Salvatore, who gave her a friendly smile.

"We're here to see Judge Crabb," I said with all the confidence I could muster.

She cocked her head and sneered, "His Honour is at his office, call his secretary and make an appointment like everyone else." She attempted to close the door, but Salvatore rammed against it with his shoulder. The impact made a loud thud as it bounced off the back wall. The woman screamed as she tumbled backwards, landing in a tangled mess on the floor.

In seconds, Salvatore was on her. He slammed his hand on her mouth, shutting her up. I closed the door behind us as I stepped inside, mesmerised, petrified, and exhilarated.

Salvatore pinned the woman, pushing her head onto the cold marble floor. One of her high heels had fallen off in the struggle, the other heel scraped the floor as she tried to regain her perch. She struggled and cried against Salvatore's grip.

He remained calm, just holding her, watching her face as large, fat tears rolled down her reddening cheeks.

"Shhhhh," he calmed her, the sound filling the hallway with unease. Her struggle seized.

"We are not going to hurt you. Nod if you understand," her head bounced against the floor as she bobbed.

"Good," Salvatore continued. "Is there anyone else here with you?"

She shook her head her eyes widening.

"Excellent." Salvatore kept his hold on her, "We're just here to talk to your husband. Do you understand?" She nodded again.

"Now, I'm going to release you, would you like that?" She nodded; her tears pooled on the marble. "But if you scream, I'll hurt you. Real bad. Do you understand?" She whimpered her understanding. Salvatore smiled and released her. Her body sagged against the floor and she sucked in deep breaths, heavy tears rolling down her cheeks.

"What do you want?" Her voice was hoarse and she rubbed her neck.

"Like I said, darling, we just want to talk to your husband," he offered her his hand, "Stand up."

She ignored his hand and pushed herself up against the wall, squaring her shivering frame. He smirked at her bravery.

"Let's go sit down. Why not show us your lovely dining room?"

She turned to walk away when Salvatore slid his arm into hers. Her back stiffened but she didn't fight him as she hobbled through the hallway, her single heel echoing on the marble. We walked into a modern dining room. It felt sterile —white and cold—everything felt uninviting, jagged and sharp. Uncomfortable steel seats surrounded a shiny, white table that looked more plastic than wood. Salvatore nodded over to the floor to ceiling windows. I approached each in turn and closed the curtains. They were heavy and didn't seem to belong in the room.

I felt like those curtains.

"Sit down," Salvatore pulled out a chair, and she fell into it. Her eyes darted from me to Salvatore, like a frightened deer. She wiped her tears away and adjusted in her seat.

Salvatore loomed over her, his eyes piercing, "I'm going to go call your husband and you're gonna sit here nicely while my friend looks after you. If you move, he will hurt you. If you scream, he will hurt you. If you do anything that you're not supposed to do, *we* will hurt you. Do you understand?"

Her yes was a whisper as new tears rolled down her face. Salvatore turned away and disappeared into another room. It was just me and her. Her chest rose and fell as she struggled to breathe normally, tears continued to roll down her cheeks despite her constant wiping. Her face was a mask of despair, and her fear bounced off the walls and into my curdling stomach.

Despite the initial thrill, the reality of what we were doing began to set in. I wasn't ready. I wasn't ready to hurt people, to break them, to propel them into the darkness. Funny, you never consider your soul being a casualty until you burn pieces of it away with your actions.

"You're not going to get away with this." Her eyes blazed as she found a reserve of courage. I didn't answer her, I just stood waiting.

Salvatore came back into the room, and he pulled out the chair right next to Mrs. Crabb. He gave her another charming smile, which I am sure under different circumstances would have had an entirely different effect on her, "Your husband is on his way home; this will all be over soon." She flinched as he patted her exposed thigh. Salvatore snickered. This was a side of Salvatore I always knew existed but had never seen. It scared me more than I cared to admit.

Back then I would have never been able to go against him. "What's your name sweetheart?"

"Don't call me sweetheart," she grumbled, then paled as his fingers clutched her thigh and squeezed, "What's your name?"

"Elise." She bit her lower lip as Salvatore released her and leaned back into his chair.

"Okay Elise, we are just gonna sit here, nice and calm, and wait for your husband."

She nodded.

We waited.

The room felt oppressive, the dimmed space feeling hot under the artificial lights.

The arrival of the honourable George Crabb was marked by his screeching tyres and slamming car doors.

His keys jingled in the front door and panicked voice echoed through the house, "Elise, Elise!"

"We're in the dining room." Her voice quivered.

The judge's face poked from behind the wall, his eyes bulged in his red face, his body tense and rigid. His eyes flashed between the three of us, finally landing back on Elise, "Are you okay?"

Relief washed her face and fresh tears fell from her eyes, "I'm fine."

"Did they hurt you?"

She shook her head, sniffing around her quiet sobs.

"Now that we have made sure everyone is fine, why not join us Mr. Crabb?" Salvatore started, his body lax against the seat.

"It's Your Honour."

"Yes, my mistake. Your Honour," Salvatore smirked, "Why don't you sit down?" He gestured to the free seat. Like his wife, the judge took a couple of uncertain steps and sat down. The four of us sat in a cold silence. It all felt oddly civilised.

The judge regained some of his composure. He gave me a humourless smile. The flash of disdain in his eyes did not go unnoticed, "Well gentlemen, would you care to tell me who you are and what can I do for you?"

"Well, Mr Crabb," I started.

"Your Honour!" He cut me off, his rebuke dripping irritation.

"Excuse me, Your Honour. You have something that I want, and I believe I have something that you want. I'm here to propose a trade."

"You can't possibly have anything that I want. You're a kid, a nothing, a no one," The judge sneered, not trying to conceal his contempt. He searched my face, his eyes studied mine, taking note of every detail until his mouth shrank back and any signs of mirth disappeared, "You are that runt Tony had living in his garage."

I sat unmoved by his attempt at mockery. See, I already felt the air change and fear creep into the room as Tony's name was mentioned. Until I made my own, I would benefit from his big, dead shadow.

"What do you want?"

"I want 72 Hill Street."

His eyes became slits, "That piece of shit concrete slab in the industrial area? Why?"

"That's none of you concern."

"Who the fuck do you think you are, thinking I'll give you anything at all?" His voice rose and a red tint decorated his features.

"Because," I took a step forward, "Tony left me an inheritance."

At my words the colour drained from his face, his anger dissolved into fear. He fell back into his chair, his hands clutching the steel arms.

"Indeed," he cleared his throat finding his voice, "What will we be trading?"

"I will return your intellectual property over to you."

The Judge nodded, hesitant, "All of it?"

I tipped my head, wondering how many offences Tony gathered on tape, "I will give you everything. You'll be free."

"George?" Elise flayed him with an incredulous look, "What are they talking about? What intellectual property? What is this really about?"

"It's alright Elise, just do what they ask and let me deal with these men." He brushed her off.

"It doesn't sound like nothing George. What are you involved with?"

"Just shut up woman!" He hissed at her and she jerked back into her seat.

At that, Salvatore's mouth curled.

"That's no way to speak to a lady," He eyed the judge, who ignored the comment.

Judge Crabb thought for a long moment his courage returning, "No deal."

"No problem," I gave him my most charming smile, while Salvatore stood up and pulled out a Glock 45 from his belt, the silencer screwed on, glinting in the light. With a steady, practiced hand, he pointed it at Elise. She cowered at the sight of it, fresh tears pooling in her eyes. The judge recoiled into his seat, his nostrils flaring.

Salvatore pushed the steel into her temple. She whimpered. He traced his hand along her neck, her lip quivered and she began to sob. Salvatore's hand trailed the length of her neck, reaching the fabric of her buttoned-up blouse and with a forceful yank he tore at the material. The shirt fell open and wilted away from her chest, revealing a black, lace bra. Elise uttered a muffled scream that stuck in her throat. Judge Crabb grabbed the table, his body vaulting from the chair. In a swift movement Salvatore swung the gun over to his direction. The cock of the hammer returned an uneasy silence to the room.

"You don't have to trust me, Mr. Crabb. But you should believe me when I tell you that before Salvatore here kills your wife, he's gonna fuck her real hard and real good, and you're going to watch as she screams your name and cries. And then, we're going to wait for your daughter to come home…what's her name again? Leora?"

Elise's sobs grew, her body shook, "Not Leora." She was begging. Salvatore placed a hand on her shoulder and squeezed. She squirmed under his touch but closed her mouth.

Judge Crabb clutched the table, his knuckles white, his face red.

In all honesty, I felt like shit. The words stung my mouth as I said them, but I needed that fucking property, and he needed to give it to me.

At any cost.

I continued.

"After that, we might just show them all your videos," Elise flashed a look over to the judge, "By tomorrow morning the media will be feasting on the carcass of what used to be your career."

Crabb's eyes bore into me, his body trembled. I wasn't entirely sure if it was fear or rage. Probably a combination of both.

Elise kept asking what we were talking about, George shut her up with a look. He sat back wiping the back of his hand against his forehead, "Alright. Alright, stop. Sit back down and we can talk about this."

"There's nothing more to talk about. You need to draw up papers and sign the property to my shell company. I want it done by the end of the day." My heart hammered and a surge of power flooded my veins. I have to admit I loved the rush, watching him cower, argue, break down bit by bit. It was exhilarating, fascinating, addictive.

"It doesn't work like that, it takes time…"

"You don't have any." I held his gaze.

He clenched his jaw, his face tormented, twisting to anger, hopelessness and finally resignation, "Fine."

"Excellent. I knew you were a reasonable man. Be back here at five o'clock. Have the papers drawn up by then."

"You fucking asshole," He hissed through gritted teeth.

"I might be an asshole, but I wasn't stupid enough to trust Tony."

"You're worse than Tony. That fat bastard promised me there was going to be no evidence."

I scoffed, "Tony promised a lot of people a lot of things." The Judge nodded bitterly. "Now let me make you a promise. If you call anyone and discuss our meeting, our deal is off. If the paper work isn't done by five o'clock, the deal is off. If you try and fuck me in anyway, your family will suffer in ways you can't begin to imagine."

"Stay away from my family. I'll have everything ready by tonight, bring the tapes."

"You best be alone."

"I'm a reasonable man."

"I'm not."

"I'll do what you asked, just leave my family alone." I held his gaze across the dining room table.

"Alright. Let me walk you to your car. You'll have a very busy day at the office." The judge stood up, his legs unbalanced. I wrapped my hand around his shoulders and he flinched at the touch. I lead him toward the hallway, "Salvatore here will keep Elise company until five o'clock. Everything best be in order. See you later, Your Honour." His eyes burned with hatred as we stepped out of the room.

He shook away from me, then hurried to the front door. The engine of his car came to life, followed by screaming wheels, which faded as he drove away.

I returned to the dining room where Salvatore sat, gun in hand, facing Elise.

"Can we trust him?"

His eyes flicked to Elise and he nodded.

"I need to get back to work…"

"As we discussed," Salvatore cut me off.

I took one last look at Elise, and tried to reassure her that it would all be okay as long as her husband followed the instructions.

Elise nodded and whimpered, her sobs filling the room. She straightened her back and pulled her shirt closed. Her perfect hair had come apart, flyways stuck to her sweaty scalp. Her cheeks were stained in black mascara. The perfectly manicured woman who had opened the door had withered away in less than an hour.

"See you tonight." Salvatore cocked his head in response, his eyes glued to the broken woman before him.

I stepped outside and didn't look back. I was barely holding myself together, my body was on fire, tingling. A mixture of excitement and fear surged through me. My stomach suddenly gripped my body in a tight squeeze, and all I wanted to do was vomit, and fly, and be someone else, be somewhere else, and pretend none of this was happening.

***

I was sick with anticipation for the rest of the day. I snapped and shouted and threatened over the simplest mistakes. Over nothing. My angst grew with every ticking second. The clock like a pendulum inside my mind, ticking away the time, burning away the fuse.

Tick, tock.

By four o'clock, I was all but unravelling. My stomach jumped and tossed like a ship on a stormy sea. I drowned the feeling in the shower.

At four thirty, Romeo arrived. Salvatore and Romeo had history, that's all I knew. I also knew he looked similar enough to me, similar enough he could have almost been me. Almost.

He knocked on the office door, wearing a cheap smile and a cheaper suit. His head was covered by a baseball hat that hung low over his face.

He stepped inside and closed the door behind him, "Salvatore told me to be here."

I nodded and stood from behind my chair, "Strip."

I unbuttoned my shirt and pulled off my pants. Romeo did the same, handing over his clothes. Despite our similarities, the shirt pulled up along my wrists and the pants felt too short, and too tight against my waist. I grimaced, smelling his pharmacy discount cologne as the fabric made my skin itch.

"Did Salvatore walk you through procedures?"

Romeo nodded and clapped a hand on my shoulder, "I've got this covered kid, now go take care of business."

It was somewhere between mockery and motivation. No one took me seriously. Not yet.

I stepped out of his touch and gave him a long, lingering look. He rounded my desk and sat down, ignoring me. The computer screen came to life and a minute later half naked women were on the screen. I left the office.

I sucked in a steadying breath, hoping I looked as casual as Romeo had walking into my office ten minutes before. The baseball cap lay low across my face, and I hoped it hid my clenched jaw. I stuffed my hands into the pants pockets so they would hide the too-short shirt and my fidgeting fingers. I walked, fighting my body, reminding myself to stay calm, stay cool, keeping my strides measured, thoughtful. My entire body screamed as I casually walked away from the car wash and the men watching it.

I slipped on my gloves and entered the judge's house at one minute before five. My forehead was covered in nervous sweat and my stomach fought the urge to lurch. Exactly a minute after that, the judge walked into his house, carrying a suitcase and a heavy expression. His eyes narrowed as he saw me.

"Good evening Your Honour."

"Go fuck yourself."

I smirked as I led him into the dining room.

Salvatore sat on the same chair where I had left him earlier that morning. Elise was now dressed in a cream business suit. She sat silently. Her makeup reapplied, her face grey in the lights.

"Elise—" The judge started, but I cut him off.

"Let us conclude our business." Judge Crabb shot me an icy look and lifted his briefcase, slamming it onto the table. The clang of metal on metal elicited a yelp from Elise, who shot her husband a look of indignation.

He clicked the briefcase open and pulled out a number of papers and a black pen, which he clicked before turning his attention to me.

"You will have to sign."

The signature wasn't mine, it belonged to a Mr. Kevin Brown, the owner of a shell company in the Bahamas. Needless to say, I was Kevin Brown. But, anyone looking for me would be taken through an endless wormhole of false leads and never-ending paperwork. I now owned a dilapidated, broken-down building that housed Tony's millions.

I signed and initialled and collated the paperwork. The judge placed the documents in three separate envelopes, each already postmarked to various institutions that would make the transaction legal and swift. He handed me the bundle of papers, "I didn't think you would trust my secretary to post them out in the morning."

I snatched the envelopes from him while Salvatore stood up. Swift and quite, he rounded the table till he stood directly behind Elise.

"Now where are my tapes?"

Even as he spoke, we both caught the flash of Salvatore's

gun as he plunged it against the back of Elise's head and pulled the trigger. The bullet shot from her forehead, leaving behind a singed black mark and a trickle of blood.

Everything happened very slowly and simultaneously very fast.

At the flash of the gun, I lunged at the judge who leapt from his chair. I grabbed his shoulders and knocked him back into the chair, Salvatore already walking towards us, his gun pointed at judge Crabb's face.

"We had a deal," He snivelled as Salvatore's gloved hand placed the gun into Judge Crabb's own. With an ironclad grip, he forced the Judge to twist his wrist, and stuffed the barrel into his mouth. His protest was mute and pathetic as he gurgled on the gun. The muffled shot erupted and a splash of bloodied brain matter covered the back wall.

Salvatore released his grip and allowed the hand to fall. The gun fell from it with a clang.

"Let's go."

Salvatore gripped me by the arm and pulled me to the door. Bile rose in the back of my throat. It burned vile and sour, and my body shook as it tried to expel the images, the smell of the acrid gunpowder and metallic blood. My body lurched and Salvatore propelled me forward.

Away.

Pushing.

Pulling.

Urging.

He released me when we were two blocks away.

I turned to face him, my heart hammering my chest, "You killed them, you fucking killed them." I could feel the panic rise with the bile.

"Shut your mouth."

"What did you do? That wasn't part of the plan. You weren't supposed to…" my voice fell away.

"To what?" He cut me off his face contorted, "Say it."

"Kill them." It was a choked whisper as my stomach twisted.

"They would have talked. It would've been all be over."

"But…"

"No buts kid." Salvatore pushed me against a wall with the full force of his body. His hand came up to my throat and it threatened to spill the contents of my stomach on him.

"Now boy, swallow that fear down. Swallow the nerves and disgust. Swallow your anger and let it burn inside you," He squeezed tighter and I forced a swallow, "If you want to survive, to lead, you keep all that shit buried deep, deep down. You learn, right now, tonight. No emotion, no regret. No turning back."

I swallowed again and pulled air into my lungs, shutting my eyes against the image that will forever be seared into my mind. Death was now part of me, and I had to accept him. I opened my eyes and locked eyes with Salvatore.

"Get the fuck off me." It was a strangled grated sound.

"Make me." He didn't move. He didn't squeeze or fight or push, he just stood there challenging me, ushering me over the threshold.

I grabbed his wrist and pulled up, then yanked it down and away from my neck. I stood to my full height and looked down into Salvatore's eyes. The storm in his eyes raged as he nodded and smiled, "Just like that."

We made our way back to his car and back to the car wash. My days as a kid were over.

She was silent for a long time.

Too long.

That length of time that gnaws at you and brings all the wrong kinds of questions crawling from the dark recesses of your mind.

"Mia?" She flinched at her name, as if I had struck her, and my heart plummeted. It was reaching terminal velocity and would smash against the vast emptiness of my soul and shatter.

A single heavy tear slid down her cheek and her mouth quivered. She cleared her throat, "All I can think about are those kids."

I chewed the inside of my lip. I knew those images. I carried them with me like ink on my soul, all while she had but an inkling, an idea. I could feel her pain, the rawness of it cut through me.

"I know you think you're a monster, Gabriel, but you're wrong. They made you who you are, and you chose to be better than all of them."

"Mia…"

"I've been so blind, I didn't know…"

"Mia?"

"It's going to be ok, Gabriel."

"What are you talking about?"

She took my hand in hers and placed it over her heart letting the sheet fall away, her naked flesh searing my hand.

"I understand now. Forgive yourself."

My heart slammed in my chest. *Forgiveness?* I didn't deserve any.

As if reading my thoughts Mia leaned into me, her lips grazing mine ever so softly. I groaned at the feel of her warmth. My face leaned against hers, our breaths mingled, our hands holding on to one another, holding on to the last grain of sanity.

"Forgive yourself, Gabriel." She breathed it into me like one breathes life into the dying.

I gripped her, my body craving her warmth, needing her comfort.

I held her. Like holding on to dear life. I have opened myself bare to her and still she accepted it. Accepted me.

The bed tilted and shifted around us as we fell into it.

Us.

It was a first for me. To be an us. No even as a kid, never with Alice. We were never an *us*, we were never a family. It was just Alice and me. Now, with Mia, I became a part of something. Something bigger than myself. I became part of an expanded universe, and I never wanted to leave.

I pulled her close to me. I may never be able to forgive myself but I need to know without a doubt that she would forgive me.

My mouth crashed into hers, seeking forgiveness in her full, trembling lips. Begging for absolution as I captured her mouth with hungry urgency, reclaiming her, possessing her, pleading with her. I could feel her uncertainty, it radiated from her in a scorching heat, even as she kissed me. Despite her words, she hadn't forgiven me. Not yet.

I broke away from her, fell off the bed and to my knees, pulling her legs off the edge. When it came to Mia, I had no problems begging for forgiveness.

I lay a single, soft kiss on her knee. I lay another on the outside of her thigh. A third, a little higher up. My mouth peppered her legs with kisses, my hands forcing her to part them for me as I kissed her inner thighs, grazing her skin with the bristles of my growth, leaving soft red reminders of my being there. Her eyes fell closed, and her chest fell and rose at my touch.

"Please forgive me, luce mia," my hands slid up her ass and squeezed the delicate skin. She remained silent at my pleas.

I could smell her want, potent and fervent. I kissed the glistening lips of her sex and inhaled her. "Forgive me," I sighed into her, as my tongue flicked along her. She purred, her fingers scratching my scalp. My tongue fluttered around her, as I begged for mercy, beseeching her with my tongue as it traced the words around her wetness.

I paused as she shivered, "Do you forgive me Mia?"

Her silence forced me back as I tormented her, keeping her close but never letting her finish, watching her wage a war against me—against herself—shivering under my pleas, bending under her own will.

She quivered and shook like a leaf above me, and once again I pulled away. An agonised moan tore from her mouth.

"Gabriel." Her nails dug into, my scalp.

"Do you forgive me, mia luce?"

"Yes," her beautiful face was tortured and flushed, "But you need to forgive yourself."

I kissed her again, my tongue flicking its own brand of retribution, thanking her for my absolution—worshiping, devoting—until she crashed around my mouth in pure joy. Her hips grinding against my mouth, taking, forgiving, accepting; making that sound that lies somewhere between pain and pleasure. It was desperation and deprivation and utterly devastating. All I wanted was to bottle it up and keep it forever.

When she settled, I placed a single kiss between her legs, enjoying the shudder, "Thank you for forgiving me."

"There's nothing to forgive, Gabriel." She gave me a smile that was almost shy, and my heart ruptured with ache. She was exquisite. She looked at my bulging erection, and when she said nothing, I knew my forgiveness came at a price. I sucked in a deep breath and stood up. My eyes roamed her body.

Her eyes glazed over in the place where ecstasy lived. Happiness. I wanted to give it to her. But not here.

"Where do you want to go?"

"What?" She lifted herself off the bed on an elbow, her wild hair fell across her face.

"You said you wanted to run away, to go somewhere. Where do you want to go?"

"I've never been anywhere." She scrunched her face as she thought about it.

"Anywhere."

Her nose twitched as she thought, "I want to go to Paris."
"Why?"

"Cause people say it's the city of love," she gave me a wicked grin and licked her top lip.

I growled, my cock twitching, "Paris is cold this time of year. I want to take you somewhere where the sun is shining, and I can watch you run around in a bikini all day."

"All day?" She bit her lower lip and fluttered her eyelids.

I lunged at the bed and she scrambled away from me shirking. I stalked her, climbing above her in a slow measured pace, feeling her skin beneath me. She taunted me with her eyes and glossy lips.

When we were face to face, her cheek grazed mine as she whispered in my ear, "I want you to take me."

"Where?"

"Everywhere." I knew she wasn't talking about anywhere on a map.

I hovered at her entrance, heat radiating from everywhere.

There was a knock at the front door that echoed through the penthouse. Our heads turned in unison to the empty living room beyond.

"Who is that?"

"Only one other person has the code to the elevator."

My forehead fell against her chest as the knocking turned into pounding, "He never comes up here." I gave her an apologetic smile and climbed off searching for my boxers.

Salvatore stood stoic at the door; his face blank.

"Sorry to interrupt boss, but we need to talk," His eyes roamed my naked torso and bulging boxers, "I wouldn't have interrupted if it wasn't important."

I sighed and nodded, my body craving Mia's heat.

"What is it?"

Salvatore looked around the room, "I think we better go downstairs."

"This better be fucking good Salvatore."

"I have something to show you."

"What?"

"It's outside."

"Sal…"

"Outside," He turned and was already heading to the elevator.

I ran to the room and grabbed my pants and shirt and apologised to Mia.

"I'll be right back." I ran out as she huffed in disappointment.

I caught up to Salvatore, hopping as I slid legs into pants and arms into sleeves, irritated and agitated as the feeling in my pants became more uncomfortable, and my mind lingered on Mia's mouth and how close I was to—

Salvatore exited the elevator and walked out through the foyer and lobby, ignoring everyone. He crossed the road then stood waiting for me. I looked around, uncertainty creeping in.

I reached Salvatore and he put his finger to his mouth. I nodded as he put his hand in his pocket, then produced a small boxy item with wires hanging out on one side. I took it in my hand and examined it, then threw it on the ground and stood on it crushing it beneath my weight.

"Where did you find it?"

"That one was in the kitchen. It was very well hidden—too well—which is why we didn't see it. But I have no idea how long it's been there or how many more are inside."

"You think there are more?"

"I'm sure of it."

"Tell me?

"Boss…"

"Just spit it out Salvatore."

"Mia—"

I cut him off with a shove, lifting his large frame against the brick wall.

"Don't," I hissed at him.

"She's the only new person in our midst."

I winced at the truth in his words.

Fuck.

I set him down, digesting his words. I cradled my head in my hands, "Are you sure?"

"No, I'm just stating facts."

I nodded trying to push through the doubt that was rising inside me. None of it made sense.

"What do you want to do, boss?"

"I want you to stop fucking calling me that Salvatore," I clenched my fists and shut my eyes trying to think,

"Someone is listening. They want information so we'll give it to them. Then we disappear for a while and let them chase ghosts. Go to the shop, buy two first class tickets to Paris for Sunday. Make sure that when you buy the tickets, you speak loudly and clearly. Make sure you give them all the details."

He nodded as I spoke, Salvatore smiled and cocked his head.

"Call the boys, you know what to do."

"No problem."

Salvatore looked down for a second and grabbed my arm as I turned away, "Be careful boss."

I shook his hand away and crossed the road, heading back inside.

A feeling of unease settled inside me as I wondered who had been listening to me. To us. How had I let this happen? Let all my defences down and allowed an intruder into my home. My stomach clenched with uncertainty. Mia. I shook away the thought, disgusted I would even consider it.

When I entered the penthouse, she was dressed again. She looked up from the book she was reading as if I had caught her doing something she shouldn't have. The feeling made my heart sink.

"What was that about?"

"Business."

She raised an eyebrow waiting for more. I shook my head, brushing her question off.

"You don't trust me?"

"Of course I do. It's just…" there was no way to finish that sentence. I dragged a hand through my hair and took a step closer, "I wanted it to be a surprise."

"What?" Her eyes grew wide, and her mouth pulled into an excited grin.

My lips twitched at the sight of her, my heart panged with the lie, "We're going to Paris."

"We are?" She squealed and fell into my arms, her lips

seeking mine. Her devastating kiss, hungry and deep. My hips finding hers, grinding, and seeking

She broke away, "Not now, I have to pack." I grunted in desperation and released her knowing I was going to suffer.

If only I knew how much.

I remembered why I hated public places. There were too many places to hide, too many faceless people that I couldn't see coming. The airport was packed with the usual manner of people who exuded too much happiness. With Mia by my side, I could have almost been one of them. Almost.

I could feel eyes on me, even if I couldn't quite work out where they were or who they belonged to. We were being watched, and we were going to play the game right till the very end.

Mia kept looking behind her; maybe my paranoia rubbed off on her. I winged an arm around her and lead her towards security.

"Don't worry, you're safe with me." I hoped it sounded convincing.

We lined up at the customs counter. Lines, endless lines and permeated stink, chatter and colour—too much, too close. Most people feel safe in a crowd, I just felt exposed.

The passport control clerk flipped through my passport. He read over my name and his eyes grew a few inches in their sockets. He glared at me, straightening his back, and looked from the picture to my face. I gave him my best smile, feeling Mia's nervous jittering next to me.

"One minute, sir." His hand crawled along the wooden panel of his booth. I knew he was searching for a button. Mia gasped next to me, and I tightened my hand around her.

A moment later a man walked over to the booth, and the

two men held a whispered conversation. They eyed me, then Mia, and the older of the two grabbed our passports and stood in front of us.

"Hello sir, madam. Would you follow me please?"

I stared at the man, his forehead creased like and old hundred dollar note, "What seems to be the problem exactly?"

"Would you please follow me?"

"Why?"

Mia's eyes darted around as people's heads turned, and they began to stare, "Let's just go please."

She shook away from my grasp and took a step forward, indicating that we would follow wherever we were being taken.

The little scene had brought more security guards into the room, they were eyeing me suspiciously.

The older man led us into a corridor. The once white paint, crawled away from the wall in greying corners, and the ceiling lights hung too low, showing off all the imperfections on carpets and doors. The corridor smelt like jet fuel and over brewed coffee.

We walked by a number of closed wooden doors with names stencilled across them.

We stopped in front of an office door. The title 'Immigration agent Daniel Reynolds' hung in black letters, whose corners were peeling off with age. He closed the door behind us as we stepped inside.

"Please sit." He gestured to the two chairs in front of his desk, and Mia dropped into one, her face drawn, her mouth downturned.

He held our passports, examining the pictures, "Gabriel D'Angelo?"

"In the flesh."

"We've been waiting for you." I heard Mia's strangled gasp as her eyes shot to me.

"Good. So, everything's organised?"

"Yes sir." Mia did a double take as she flipped between me and Daniel. I ignored her.

"The plane?"

"Is waiting for you."

"Our passports?"

He fumbled with the booklets in his hand, "Of course." He reached for the stamps on his desk and, with two thuds, pressed them into our passports and placed them in my waiting hand.

"Thank you." With that, I put my hand out to Mia who still looked as if she had been slapped in the face.

"What's going on Gabriel?" I could hear the note of agitation.

"I'll explain on the plane, but right now we need to go."

"Not till you tell me what's going on."

So.

Fucking.

Stubborn.

I dragged my fingers through my hair and locked eyes with Mia, "I can throw you over my shoulder and carry you, or you can just trust me. Either way Mia, you're coming with me."

Her eyes burned into mine, and I was losing my patience when she finally placed her hand in mine and allowed me to pull her from the chair. I sighed internally hoping the relief wasn't obvious on my face.

I turned back to Daniel who stood awkwardly, pretending to look at a spot on the floor, "Which way?"

"Down the corridor and to the left. Kylie is expecting you."

"Thank you," I flashed him a smile.

"Safe travels Mr. D'Angelo, miss."

We marched down the corridor. My hand at the small of Mia's back, urging her forwards.

Kylie was a skinny thing that looked like she lived off a diet of leaf shakes and yoga. Her thin, muscular arms hung like branches from her tight singlet that was tucked into a knee length black skirt. A pin with wings fixed above her flat chest, and her black hair stretched behind her in a tight bun.

She smiled as we approached.

"Sir, Ma'am. I'm Kylie and I'll be your hostess on this trip. I understand you are anxious to be on your way. So, if you'll follow me, we can board right away and get going."

We stepped into a massive hanger. The imposing structure clung onto the hot air, making the space stifling despite its size. My Bombardier Global Express gleamed in the morning light as someone slid open the doors. They creaked and moaned and a slight wind swirled inside, carrying with it the smell of Avgas.

It was hard not to get excited seeing the beautiful machine waiting, anticipating. Its engine fuelled, its parts working, all wanting to ignite and take flight.

Kylie climbed the stairs and joined two perfectly manicured men who stood waiting. Their uniforms ironed within an inch of their lives, shirts pressed and starched, golden bars decorated their shoulders. The men shook our hands and introduced themselves as the captain and co-captain. They smiled and joked about blue skies and smooth sailing, then turned into the cockpit and closed the door behind them.

Kylie ushered us into the body of the plane. We stepped inside. My chest ached as Mia gasped, her expression hovering somewhere between amazed and perplexed.

The plane was spacious, plush and spotlessly clean. It smelt like money and overindulgence. Kylie stepped around us, "Follow me please."

The room consisted of four leather seats, two on each end of the cabin facing one another, and a round table sat in the middle. Kylie showed us to our seats.

"Good afternoon. Once again, my name is Kylie and I'll be

your hostess for the duration of your flight. If you could fasten your seatbelts, I'll inform the pilot that we're ready for take-off."

I could hear the click of Mia's belt as I clicked mine. Kylie stepped out of the room, and Mia's gaze fell on my face, "What's going on Gabriel? Where are we going?"

Before I could answer, Kylie returned and the plane stuttered and began to move. Sunlight flooded the cabin as we breached the hanger.

"Good afternoon, this is your captain speaking. We're awaiting clearance from the tower and will be taking off momentarily. Kylie, please secure the cabin for take-off." The speakers fell silent.

Kylie gave us a quick safety demonstration, pointing out the whereabout of the toilets, bedroom and emergency exit.

I didn't miss the slight parting of Mia's mouth as Kylie mentioned a bedroom. I wanted to take her there right then and fuck that expression right off her face, fuck her till the plane reached altitude.

"Can I offer you a drink for take-off?"

"Whiskey, on the rocks." I looked to Mia inviting her to partake.

She shook her head and Kylie stepped away.

"Gabriel." She was getting annoyed.

I smirked at her, "Just sit back and relax. I'll tell you everything you need to know just as soon as we stop getting interrupted." Even as I spoke, Kylie came in and handed me the whiskey.

"Please be sure to remain seated as we take off," Kylie smiled broadly and stepped out of view.

The engine whined as the plane rolled up the tarmac. Sunlight spilled inside through the small windows, and I found myself staring at Mia.

Despite herself, she sank into the lavish chair and her face fell into a trance as we rolled along the black tar. In minutes, the engine whined in a high-pitched scream and my body shrank into the chair with the force. Mia's mouth dropped open slightly and her eyes grew wide as she stared out of the window. Whatever she saw filled her face with wonder.

We broke through a bank of clouds, and the world vanished under a blanket of white chased by brilliant blue as far as the eye can see. The engines relaxed into a purr, and Mia pried her eyes away from the window.

On cue, Kylie returned to the cabin, "Lunch will be served momentarily. Can I freshen up your drink?"

I shook my head, "Hold lunch, and give us some privacy please."

Kylie regarded me with a look that said she's seen it all, and she understood, "Just press the call button when you need anything." She tipped her head and turned in a practiced manner and strode out of the cabin, closing the doors behind her.

"Gabriel—"

"The Maldives."

"What?"

I sucked down the last of the whiskey that remained in my glass and put it down, "We're going to the Maldives"

"What, why are we going there? What happened to Paris, and what was that whole charade at the airport?"

Always so many questions. I unbuckled my seatbelt and stood, looking down at Mia sprawled like a queen in the plush, leather seat.

"I wish you'd just trust me enough to tell me what's going on so I wouldn't have to find out this way."

"Of course, I trust you. I'm just trying to protect you."

"From what?"

I sighed, "I don't really know."

She arched her brows and cocked her head. God, she looked sexy when she was pissed off. "Gabriel!"

"We found bugs, all over the shop. Someone's been

listening to us, looking for something." I watched Mia, the flicker in her eye, the twitch of her fingers on her seat. "Salvatore seems to think it's Emilio Rocco. We don't know who he is or what he's capable of. But he already took you from me once, and I'm not going to give him a chance to do it again. Until I know what we're dealing with, *who* we are dealing with, this is the way things have to be."

Her brow gathered in a fierce stare, "What? Keeping me in the dark."

"Keeping you safe," I growled again.

"I am not safe when I'm blind."

"We're all blind Mia, but right now we're free."

Mia's face shifted at my words, "Free?"

"Whoever was following us, either thinks we've been detained at immigration or that we are on that plane to Paris. Besides Salvatore and this crew, no one has any idea where we're going, and they've been paid a great deal to maintain their silence."

I could see her mind turning over, mulling the information around like a cocktail.

"The Maldives?"

"Yes."

"Why?"

"It's far away from anywhere, no one will come looking. It's hot and sweaty, just how I like you."

"And here I was thinking that you were talking about the weather," she licked her upper lip and I swallowed hard.

"That too."

"Mm mm." She unbuckled her seatbelt and wandered the cabin. My eyes followed her ass as it sashayed around the body of the plane, disappearing as she explored the inner wonders of the private jet. I found myself chuckling when I heard her delighted squeal. She must have found the bedroom.

I fell back into my seat, the warm leather shifting around me.

"This plane is amazing!" Her face spread in a wide grin showing off her beautiful smile. It was as if the sun itself walked into the room. It made me giddy, an unfamiliar and terrorising feeling. I sucked in a deep breath as she walked towards the bay of seats.

"Is this your plane?"

I nodded taking in her reaction—flared nostrils, muted gasp.

"It's big." She prowled a little closer to me.

"It's big enough to do the job."

She smirked at me, "Overcompensating?"

I pulled her hand and spun her around until she fell on my lap with a yelp. Her hair tickled my face and I inhaled her scent, the green fields and sunshine that were always there. She smelt like home, like my home.

I grabbed her waist and pulled her onto me so that she leaned against my chest. Her ear glued to that place where my heart could have been, as it thumped and thudded unsteadily. Everything felt unbalanced when she was around, she was dizzying.

"Why don't you tell me?"

Her head spun and her dark eyes matched my intentions. I found her lips, full and beautiful. They beckoned to me as I captured them in my own; my tongue delighting in the sweet invasion of her mouth, savouring her taste, her warmth, her delight.

My hands wandered along her body, finding the soft flesh of her breasts, my fingers kneading her delicate, hardening nipples still blooming beneath my touch. She moaned into my mouth, and the sound unchained within me wild, delicious need.

My left hand moved down and clutched at the fabric of her skirt, drawing it up inch by agonising inch, exposing her long legs. My fingers sought out her wetness. Her breath hitched at my touch as my fingers circled and teased and danced with her hips as she moved them restlessly against my swollen erection.

"Gabriel," she whispered my name, "I want you." She kissed me, a gentle beautiful kiss, but wildness brewed beneath that gentleness and an urgent need commanded us both.

She lifted herself from me long enough so I could pull my pants to my knees. She lowered herself onto me, allowing my cock to stretch her softness. I growled as she sank against me. I clamped a hand around her, moulding her to me and, with the other hand, found her wetness—fluttering, swirling, and stroking.

She rocked above me, her knees clamped against my naked hips as I moved beneath her. With the engines purring below me and Mia shuddering above me, I watched the heavens and, in a pure moment of bliss, felt like a king.

I can tell you about the Maldives, about the translucent blue-green water, and how Mia's pale flesh grew tanned and honeyed each day we spent in the sun. I can tell you about the long, steamy nights and the hot sweaty days, but I won't because those memories are mine alone. Having Mia all to myself, I want to keep them pure, uncorrupted by everything else that followed. Sometimes the memories feel like dreams, and I wondered if they really happened.

What I will tell you is that we spent three beautiful, uninterrupted weeks soaking up the sun and one another. I soaked up her smiles and her delight, the feel of her skin and the taste of her mouth; I soaked up every little bit of Mia until I knew she was all I ever wanted to kiss and feel and taste.

But then, the fucking phone rang and once again every-thing changed.

It was another day in paradise. Mia breathless above me, her body moving like the waves in the ocean outside, undu-lating and rolling. She was covered in sweat with ragged breath, and she was absolutely fucking exquisite.

Until the phone rang.

I wouldn't have flinched, except that only one person had that phone number, and he was under very specific instruc-tions not to use it. Unless—

Our heads both snapped towards the trilling phone as the sound resonated around the room. The only unnatural sound, totally foreign and uninvited.

"Ignore it." Mia rolled above me, her hips pushing against mine driving me deeper.

My head fell against the pillow as I thrust up to meet her, "I can't," my hoarse voice sounded through gritted teeth.

Unrelenting, Mia swayed above me like the soft breeze that came through the window.

The phone rang.

She rolled.

It rang.

She pounded.

It rang.

She moved.

The phone stopped ringing.

Mia's smile wicked as she lifted herself just to slam against me.

The phone rang.

Mia squealed as I reached for the phone and almost toppled her off me. My body coiled at the tension in my core, my building need, my aching release.

The phone rang.

Mia rocked against me, her body arching. I let the phone scream as I grabbed Mia's hips, pounding into her with fierce slamming thrusts until I was overcome with a shattering tide of delight and release. Her body drove into mine as she called out my name, her body trembling like a leaf above me.

Mia fell at my side, our breaths and sweat mingled. Our bodies reached and touched for the other, insatiable, unable to remain without the other.

The phone rang again.

"Fuck."

"Guess you better get it." Mia kissed me, a long gentle kiss. I watched as she rose from the bed, her perfect ass heading to the bathroom. When she slammed the door behind her, I found the receiver again.

"Hello?" It was strangled and forced.

"Are you fucking kidding me?"

"Sorry, we were—"

"I don't give a fuck," Salvatore cut me off. "You need to come home. Now."

"What's happened?"

"It's Simone." At the sound of her name a cold spear of fear pierced my heart. I scrambled up, my entire body stiffening with the cold sensation.

"Is she ok?"

"No, I don't know how much longer she can fight. If you want to say goodbye, get on your fancy plane and get yourself here. Now."

"What happened?"

"There was a fire."

"Accidental?'

"No."

"Spots?" My heart leapt at the question.

"Is with me."

My body sagged with relief, "I'm on my way."

The line went dead.

My pulse hammered in my veins. Simone. The mother I never had; the nurturing, sweet woman who took in two

broken boys and gave them both hope. My lungs clenched
and my throat closed as I fell out of the bed and grabbed my
clothes. Mia was already packing up. I had to get back to
Simone. Was it too late to save her?

Time, that callous bitch, always taunted me with the
slowing down of her movements. Everything felt as though it
was taking too long, every sensation of dread and fear saturated itself into my bones, and I drowned in the murky soup
of doubt and self-loathing.

Simone.

PART XV

The plane took off into the blackened sky—black like the curtain closing in around my heart, black like the fear that settled inside the pit of my stomach, black like the memories closing in on me.

So many memories, I sunk beneath them as the plane soared.

The death of the judge and his wife made national news. It was believed to have been a murder suicide, and the press pecked at their rotten bodies for days until all that was left were the bones picked clean; then, like the vulture they were, they moved on.

These deaths also triggered the beginning of the end for everything that I held dear. A yin and yang, a counter balance. It is true what they say, for every action there is an equal and opposite reaction.

Sometimes I still feel a niggling doubt, uncertainty about Rita's death. It wiggles around in my insides and eats away at the assurances Salvatore fed me. Was her death truly a warning, or simply retribution for Crabb and his wife?

Not a single word was written about Rita.

Salvatore dropped me off at the car wash and I shuffled

inside, my feet covered in a thin coat of white sand. All I could see was Rita's blank stare, her dead eyes bore into my soul; the image singed itself into the back of my eyelids so, that even when closing my eyes, all I could see was her.

I fell onto my bed, exhaustion blanketing my body while it clenched in agony and desperation. Wariness clutched at my bones and threatened to crack them with a swift caress. I felt the tears as they rolled silently down my face, one after the other like a deluge of pain whose gates were broken. The tears were tainted with sadness and guilt. I cried. I cried for Rita who didn't deserve her end, and I cried for myself—for the boy that never was.

I wiped my face spreading the heat along my frozen flesh. A hot white fury rose inside me. It burned, warming up the coldness like a furnace, and it beckoned me to its glow. I basked in the fury of Rita's death. I clenched my teeth, vowing her death would not be in vain, that she would not be a nameless casualty, but a soldier who fought and lost to make right what's been done wrong.

I wiped away the feeling of hopelessness and reached for Tony's books. I stared at the numbers, willing them to talk to me till something flickered in the back of my mind, something Salvatore once said about Judge Crabb. It was a sliver of an idea so thin, so vague; but I latched at it until it became a firm memory. I remembered a brief conversation between Tony and Salvatore. They mentioned the judge and joked about his tax evasion problems, and how his problems were Tony's solution to making things go away.

In a frenzy I flipped through the page and scrolled down until I found his name. Judge George Crabb. I skipped over to the next column and scanned over the letters.

M. L. PTA.

I grabbed a blank piece of paper and scrolled down the letters starting with PTA. I tapped the paper then wrote "Property Tax Evasion?"

It almost made sense, made so much sense that I went through the entire book, pulling out letters from each column and guessing—guessing notorious activities and devious behaviours. In an hour I had all the letters translated into possible offences. The list ranged from money laundering and murder, to pedophilia and the use of prostitutes.

I was clutching at straws, but the more I looked, the more it made sense. Despite the uncertainty that I had, in fact, cracked Tony's code, it felt right. For the first time since his funeral, I felt like I was making headway. Despite the exhaustion, I felt a surge of energy.

I stared at my list and gritted my teeth. Each of the men listed there were vile and each would pay. I vowed it then and there. They would pay for Rita's death, because they each had a hand in it. Every secret was a slice on her beautiful skin, every offence a bruise, every lesion a violation of her most precious of places.

I searched the numbers. Unlike the letters, I still couldn't find a pattern. Until I could, I scolded myself for my stupidity.

I grabbed a long black hoodie and pulled on my shoes. Then I ran.

The phone booth had been on that corner for as long as I had; a derelict and neglected thing, much like the boy who used to stare at the numbers, wondering if he punched enough of them if Alice would pick up on the other end.

I stepped into what was left of the booth, the glass had broken years ago and the phone book stolen. Graffiti marked every visible surface. I grabbed the receiver and dialled.

I was taking a chance that he would answer, but then again only dogs serve. Salvatore's voice was edged with anger when he heard my voice.

"Don't speak, just listen. I know Joe has people watching the shop, and I know he is there with you now. I need access to the office. I need you to tell him that I'm your cop friend, the one from last night. Tell him the police think Rita's death is suspicious, that they're coming to raid the premises, and they're bringing everyone."

"You're crazy kid." He sounded somewhere between resigned and agitated.

"I need to get into Tony's computer. It has all the answers."

"You won't have much time." He hung up, unceremoniously.

I watched the garage. My back to the wall, sinking into the late morning shadows. My heart thumped in my chest, and I could taste my anxiety—it tasted like curdled yoghurt.

The heavy iron door flew open, and from it exited a steady stream of men dressed far too well to be working in a mechanic shop. They exited like frightened ants whose hill has been flooded, walking hastily into cars and driving off. I saw Salvatore among them, he blended in like the dog he was.

I waited ten minutes, just in case. I knew someone would have been left behind to watch. I knew I'd just hung a rope around Salvatore's neck. I hurried.

I ran around the corner and scaled the back walls, keeping myself as small as I could, scanning every car and every shadow. I went in through Tony's hidden door. Only two other people knew of its existence; one of them was dead, and the other just drove off with my enemies.

They had left in a hurry. Half drank coffee mugs still stood on the table and half eaten sandwiches collapsed on deserted plates. I would have enjoyed it more if I wasn't in a hurry.

I took the stairs one at a time, my back glued to the wall, tracing the same path I did almost a week ago, when I found Tony. I walked into the office, and the memories whipped me like his belt. Tony splattering and dying in his chair, how his eyes bulged, and the way he begged me to keep him alive. Fuck that fat bastard.

I sat in the chair and shivered, then switched the computer on. The glow of the green screen cast an eerie light across the office walls.

The password request flashed on the screen. I stared at it as it blinked at me, mocking. I didn't bother trying his wife's name nor his daughters. None were precious to him.

With shaking fingers, I typed Rita's name, remembering his leers, the salvia gathering in his mouth as he looked at her. I shuddered trying to shake the disgust from my body. With each click of the keyboard I felt the agony of her death, like stabbing her all over again. When my access was denied, I felt relief. As if somehow I had freed her from him.

I searched the recess of my mind until another memory rose. My birthday, the single slice of cake while he purged on the rest of it.

I typed, my fingers hovering over the keyboard as if they were afraid to catch on fire. With each letter, the taste of the cake rose in my throat; the cream souring, the chocolate rancid, the cherries tart and bitter.

"BLACKFORREST"

The computer sprang to life. I scanned the rows of files neatly stacked in cyberspace. I read each one, searching for anything that shouldn't have been there. The files listed inventory and invoices, paycheques. On the surface it all looked like the computer of a working mechanic shop.

And then I saw it, the file was titled "fun stuff". I clicked on it and my screen exploded with thousands of pictures. Naked woman paraded their body parts in the most provocative of ways. Their beautiful curvy parts shown off. My cock twitched at the sight, throbbed at it. But I pushed it aside. This was where Tony hid his secrets, in the wide opening of these women's legs. See I knew Tony's deepest, darkest secret. I knew he didn't like women—just girls and boys.

I scrolled down hoping for a clue but found none. I started at the end. Tony flooded the file with so many women, no man would ever manage to go through them all. So, I knew it would be closer to the end. I started clicking on pictures. Tongues and teeth leered at me, nipples bounced in my face, and wet, glistening lips invited me in.

My cock surged in my pants as I flicked through the images systematically. Relishing in the pictures while simultaneously hating them.

I clicked on the image. She was a fiery redhead bent over a chair, her ass up in the air, showing off the curls on her glistening lips. Her piercing green eyes looked right at me, and she licked her fire-engine red lips. A silver halo hung over her head, and white angel wings clung to her naked shoulders.

The screen turned blue. A single white bar with a blinking cursor stared at me. I sucked in a deep breath and typed in Judge Crabb's file number, then pressed enter.

The screen went black for a second and then a recording started to play. In the corner the time flashed 12.07 pm, Friday 23/05/1993.

The camera was facing a bed. It was placed in a nearly barren room, the walls bare and ugly. The four-poster bed was made up in black sheets and red pillows. A set of handcuffs hung from each of the bed posts.

The girl that walked in had far too much makeup on. Maybe it was in an attempt to seem older. She was dressed in a mini skirt and a short leopard print cardigan that hung open over a lacy, black bra. She seemed to totter in her high heels. George Crabb followed behind her; a big, greedy smile plastered on his face. She looked young, too young, not much older than I was at the time. My belly turned at the thought.

The girl looked scared but was putting on a brave face,

smiling and teasing. His Honour appraised her with his hungry eyes and sat on the edge of the bed licking his lips.

"Take your clothes off. Slowly," he cooed to her and bile rose in my throat as she danced, peeling off the few items she had on. He beckoned her closer with a finger and she approached him, taking tentative steps.

"Closer darling, I won't bite. Much." He chuckled at his own joke and gripped her wrist, forcing her between his legs.

When his lips touched her perky, pink nipple, she grimaced. He may have read it as a smile as he sucked harder and dug his fingers into her waist, pulling her ever closer. But I know what fear and disgust look like, and it painted her face like a grotesque artwork.

He whispered sweet nothings to her as he grazed her skin with his mouth, exploring her youth. Then with a hand on her shoulder, he pushed her onto her knees and instructed her to pull off his pants and get his cock out. She obliged as he grunted with the effort.

He cupped her face in his hands and lowered her mouth to his cock, compelling her to suck. Delicate, unpractised movements at first. He groaned at her touch, his body shivering with ecstasy till he could wait no more. He fisted a clump of her hair and forced her down on his shaft; she gagged and flailed but still he pushed and pulled her until he jerked and shook, releasing himself into her mouth.

"Mm mm," he purred, "You are such a good girl." He placed his fingers under her chin, "Now get on the bed. "

Her face was red and tears pooled in her eyes. He slapped her ass as she climbed on the bed beside him.

"On your belly, sugar." She obliged as he rolled above her, clasping each of her wrists securing them with the cuffs.

He slapped her ass again and she flinched at the sting. He chuckled, enjoying her struggle.

"Now darling, I want to see that exquisite ass of yours. I

want it up in the air." She tucked her knees below her belly, and the judge gasped in appreciation.

He began her spanking. She flinched at first and then squirmed. Her moans turning into cries while his palm met the soft flesh of her ass, until tears ran from her face and her ass burned redder than the pillows.

"Yes, sweetheart. You have no idea how beautiful you are from this angle." Without warning, the judge ploughed into her arse and she howled in pain.

It was brutal and savage, and I could see his joy as he destroyed this beautiful, delicate thing. The only comfort I took away was that it ended quickly. But for her, not quickly enough.

When he was done, he fell on top of her crumpled body and sucked in long satisfied breaths while a single teardrop tumbled from her eye. It traveled along her nose and dropped onto the cushion, the blot spreading like ink in water, seeming to stain the cushion.

The time stamp of the tape showed that it continued on for 45 minutes more. I didn't watch the rest; I saw all I needed to see. Her face will haunt me like those in the photographs. Just another lost soul, another broken, fractured spirit, scared and tormented. I clenched my jaw as I vowed to get her some peace.

I exited the video and returned to the blinking white bar. Each number was a file, each held the worst graphic secrets of these vile human beings, and I almost had possession of them all. I wouldn't be able to walk out with Tony's computer without being hounded. I needed the originals.

I went back to the women. They all stared at me, leered at me, tempted me. I was running out of time, and eventually Joe's men would get tired of waiting for the cops and the charade would be over.

Tick, tock.

I scrolled through the women till I found the one I was

looking for. The red-haired woman sat on a Victorian parlour chair. It was plush and velvety red. Her long hair cascaded across her shoulders and her pink nipples peeked from among the strands. She sat back, legs spread open, inviting, enticing, and saturated. Her lips burned around her sharp teeth. The two devil horns poked above her head to complete the look. I clicked.

A list of real estate buildings appeared on the screen. Property after property. I checked through them all and made note of the only three I was unaware of. I memorised them and retraced my steps, deleting all my searches and histories. I logged off and snuck out as undetected as when I arrived.

Back at the car wash, I paced the length of my room like a caged animal, my heart pounded and my palms felt clammy as my mind reeled with all I had discovered. My mind felt blurred and my body heavy, the last three days catching up to me like a freight train without breaks. My mind was hurled with too much information like it was peppered with bullets. I fell onto the bed, sinking under the darkness.

R ough hands shook me awake. Salvatore's broken face looked down on me as I bolted up. I've never had a problem waking up. Alice made sure of that when she let us squat in illegal places, or when she brought men home with wandering hands.

The room was black. Silver moonlight and yellow street lights collided against my walls. I studied the man who loomed above me. His lip was sliced open, his cheeks swollen and bruised. His knuckles scraped and broken.

"Let's go."

I was already dressed, having fallen asleep with my shoes on. My body felt worn and tired as if I hadn't slept at all, like

I hadn't slept in years. I was falling apart at the seams, but I had to be strong—for Rita, for those kids, for that prostitute who cried on the bed. I had to finish it, to finish them.

We climbed into his car and he cocked his head towards another vehicle parked across the road. I was being watched as closely as he was. The engine roared to life and Salvatore pulled away casually, as if he hadn't a worry in the world, as if his association to me hasn't been discovered, and his face wasn't broken and his ego bruised.

In the mirrors I could see our tail. They followed at a good distance and parked three cars away in the parking lot of a well-lit bar.

The alcohol and cigarettes were the first thing I smelt; they crawled up my nose like well known acquaintances and lingered. The air was heavy with smoke and alcohol infused laughter. But, beneath the smells and the sounds I could almost feel the desperation, the loneliness of the patrons. It leached into their seats and stained the floors. The poor and the pathetic found a home, a place to feel as if they belonged. Once I could have almost been one of them. Almost.

The bar stretched over the length of the back wall and around it gathered the usual animals. Tables were scattered around the dimly lit room. I followed Salvatore to the bar. The wood sticky and worn.

The barman slapped two beers in front of us, the heads were too big, and they fizzed in the hot air, the glass sticky with spilled alcohol and clammy with condensation.

"How much do they know?" I sipped the warm beer and regretted it instantly.

Salvatore's mouth tipped at the edge, "Not enough to kill you yet, but just enough to come after everything. After tonight you'll have one, maybe two nights tops. Then you need to find a place to disappear."

I nodded, staring at the beer I wasn't going to drink and wondered how much of the content was beer and how much was piss. Salvatore didn't touch his drink, instead offering it to the inebriated man on his left. The man cheered to his health as Salvatore picked up the empty glass and placed it in front of him. After a while he repeated the process with mine.

Despite the warmth of the bar, I felt a cold spear of fear as it stabbed through me again and again. It spread around my body in waves as we sat for an hour talking about nothing. Keeping up appearances.

We waited.

A tall brunette walked into the bar, her top lip pierced and the side of her head shaved. It was dyed black. Everything about her felt artificial. She eyed Salvatore and gave him a long familiar smile as if they shared a secret. He tipped his head and her smile broadened.

"Hi, handsome."

"Roxy," he cocked his head and she licked her bottom lip at the sight of his roguish smile, "Been a long time."

"Too long." She purred across the bar.

"You busy?"

She scanned the bar, her eyes flicking over half drank beers and slumped over patrons. "Not at all," Roxy winked at him, "Bring your friend." A roar of laughter and whistles followed us as we rose from our chair and followed the woman behind the bar.

"Come on Roxy, when are you going to invite me upstairs too?" Leered one of the other men. Salvatore spun on his heels and glared at the man who quickly retreated into his drink.

Roxy led us through a narrow corridor. It was lined with empty beer crates and boxes of bar snacks.

"Hurry up, this way." She led us to a door which opened up to a back alley. It reeked of piss and garbage, fermented food and stomach contents. My own stomach heaved at the smell.

"Thanks Rox, I owe you one." Salvatore's tone was smooth and honeyed, one I had never heard before.

"Come back later this week and pay me back." She wrapped her hands around his neck and pulled him down, her lips nipping his.

He bit his lower lip as she slipped him a bunch of keys, then turned back inside and locked the door behind us. When his gaze swung back to my face, his warned me to keep my mouth shut. I smirked, then followed him to the waiting car.

The car needed a wash, black grease decorated the bonnet and oily hand prints stained the windows.

Salvatore slipped into the driver's seat and started the engine. Despite its dilapidated exterior, the interior was clean and well looked after. I lay low in my seat so that my body remained hidden. I could feel the car shift and turn, the sensation lurching through my stomach.

The radio played some classic tunes as a long silence stretched between us. We rounded a few more corners and put more distance between us and the bar before Salvatore told me I could sit up. When I did, we were on the highway, flashing lights sped by us in neon and yellows.

We drove in silence. It seemed to be this thing between us. We didn't need to talk to know what the other was thinking. There was just too much tension, too much raw pain, too much to get done to waste on words. We were both buried under clouds of thoughts and fear to worry about conversation.

⚯

The storage unit facility looked like any other—heavy, corrugated doors sealing concrete vaults. We pushed the baseball caps low over our heads and left the car parked a few streets away.

The security booth sat under a beam of light, it blazed like a bug zapper in a dark night. Insects flew above it in a delicate swarm. The echoes of TV laughter drifted from the wooden structure.

I thought of Rita and that night in the car. My body remembered the tightness and exhilaration. In the darkness, the sensations were similar except that I knew the outcome would be totally different. There would be nothing soft and beautiful, only hatred and anger that had the potential to leave a lot of bodies behind.

I pulled the cap lower on my face feeling the rush of blood as it pumped around my body in stormy waves. We approached the security booth.

The guard was lost in the whatever show he was watching, his too white teeth glowed in the light of the TV screen. His hair was shaved and his uniform showed off a muscular physique. He could have been ex-military.

Salvatore pulled out his Glock and set it behind his back as I knocked on the glass window, jerking the man out of the screen.

He eyed us, his smile fading, "Can I help you?"

"Yes hi, we are here to go look at locker seventy-three."

He flinched as if he had been bitten by a snake, "Seventy-three?"

I clenched my jaw, my body tightening, "Yes." I wondered who the locker belonged to.

The guard shifted in his chair, "I'm going to have to see some ID, please."

He reached for his keyboard and Salvatore levelled the gun with his temple, "I wouldn't do that if I were you."

The man froze, his eyes darted around like a trapped animal. He reminded me of Elise at her dining room table; the ingrained fear of the human spirit being extinguished loomed inside him.

"Give me your wallet."

"I don't have any cash man."

"Your wallet," My tone was harsh and I extended my hand out.

He jiggled in his chair, Salvatore scrutinising his every move. He shoved the wallet in Salvatore's direction.

"Tsk, tsk, tsk.," I shook my head then cocked it at Salvatore.

The guard's eyes grew wide as the butt of Salvatore's gun smashed across his face. He wailed at the pain, his hand shooting to the swelling bruise.

"Let's try that again. Give *me* your wallet." He handed me the wallet, glaring at me.

I pulled out his driver's licence and threw the wallet back into his booth.

"Now I have your address, Desmond."

The guard swallowed and said nothing, "Your wife is very beautiful."

His head spun backwards to the framed family photo on the desk; a glowing pregnant woman hugging a young boy.

"What do you want?" His shoulders slumped, the fight seeping from his body.

"The first thing you're going to do is switch off all the cameras."

"I can't d—"

"I've never had my cock sucked by a pregnant woman, have you?" I spoke to Salvatore's back.

"Never too late to try new things." He played along, his tone menacing.

"Ok, ok, just leave my family out of it." He reached for the keyboard and clicked a few commands, the bank of screens turned black, one monitor after another until only the sitcom remained, fake laughter pouring from the glowing TV.

"Master key card, please."

"Please, I'm going to lose my job."

I held out my hand, "Not if tonight never happened."

"I don't understand."

"Next time I have to ask for anything more than once, your wife will be delivering your baby on my cock."

The colour drained from his face, and he handed me a plastic card. I thanked him and ran.

I knew we had limited time, and I knew that eventually the security guard will try to get brave and everything will be fucked; mostly for him, because Salvatore would have no qualms about putting a bullet in his head. But ghosts didn't leave dead bodies behind.

I opened lockers, slapping the key card against the readers; the locks clicking and the doors lifting a mere inch off the ground to indicate they have been released. I didn't give a shit about those other lockers, I was just covering tracks. Once I was satisfied, I back tracked and returned to locker twenty three. Of course I lied to Desmond. I would never give away my only playing card.

I steadied myself then grabbed the roller door, which boomed in the night, shaking violently as if it had not been touched in years. I stepped inside, closed the door behind me, then switched the light on.

I was greeted with shelves. Three to be exact. Each was stacked with endless boxes each housing a tape. I stepped deeper into the room. The stagnant air wrapped itself around me, and I could feel it bore into my nose and slide down my throat.

I scanned the tapes, each was marked by a number. *The number.* The file numbers in his book. The numbers powerful enough to bring down half the city. In my mind, each number became a name, an offence, and a weapon. I searched for Judge Crabb, seeking his tapes. They would mysteriously fall into the presses' hands in the following week and rain down a shit storm.

I grinned at the thought and searched the shelf for one more number.

6789327.

I grabbed the tape and tucked it into my jacket pocket.

I closed the locker behind me, and returned to the booth where Salvatore stood with his gun still pointed at the guard.

"Thank you for your help, Desmond." He glared at me, hatred burning behind his eyes, "Now this is what we're going to do. You will delete tonight's log of opened lockers, and once you have done that my friend and I will leave. Nod if you understand."

He did.

I tipped my head forwards and Desmond turned in his chair and faced his computer reluctantly pushing buttons. I resisted the urge to pet him on the head and call him a good boy.

"Good. You can walk around the place and seal all the doors that popped open," I winked at him, "Feel free to look inside them, I really don't give a fuck."

He nodded again.

"You'll then bring the camera system back up and, when asked about it in the morning, say there was a system glitch. You managed to fix it, so no harm done. Do you understand?"

"Yes." Desmond's voice cracked.

"One last thing Desmond," I locked eyes with the man, "I am going to keep your licence. If anyone gets a whiff of what's happened here tonight, your family will bear the consequences. Do you understand?"

He nodded again and his eyes shone with hateful tears, "What about this?" He gestured to his swollen face.

"I'm sure you've lied to your wife before haven't you Desmond?" I smirked at him, "Tell her you were mugged on your way home, tell her that's how you lost your wallet."

He tipped his head and I placed my hand on Salvatore's shoulder, "Let's go."

We retreated. Once out of eyeshot and earshot, we jogged to the car and jumped inside. Salvatore drove us back to the bar, my heart chugged the entire trip back.

Salvatore remained silent keeping his questions to himself. I appreciated that about him, he knew how to mind his own fucking business.

He pulled back into the alley and killed the engine.

"Hold on," He stilled his hand hovering over the door handle. I dug into my pocket and produced his tape. I handed it over to him.

He took it, his eyes growing large, his mouth falling slightly open as he realised what I had given him.

"Mine?"

"As promised."

Whatever feeling overwhelmed him, he swallowed it down. I could see his entire body fighting to remain rigid, proper, hidden. "Thank you," He cleared his throat and got out of the car, tucking the tape into one of his pockets.

I cocked my head at his empty seat and followed him back into the bar.

Everything had gotten louder—the music, the people, the slurring. Salvatore ordered two beers.

When the barman placed them on the bar, he grabbed his and tipped it slightly towards me, "Salute." He called and downed the amber drink. I wasn't sure if he was lamenting or celebrating, either way the alcohol sent warmth into my body and eased the tension of the night.

When Salvatore dropped me off at the car wash, the follow car was waiting in the shadows.

Salvatore gripped my arm, "Remember what I said—a day or two max ,and then you disappear."

"For how long?"

"Just till the heat dies off—a month, maybe two."

"And then?"

"And then you can throw your match."

I wasn't meant to see Salvatore again for a while, but then Spots got hurt and I had inadvertently found a place to lay low. Simone never really knew that she didn't only save Spots' life, she also saved mine.

That night I pulled out the polaroids again. I promised the faces retribution. I needed to make their pain worth something. I vowed to make their fathers feel their pain, to ensure that anything Tony ever touched wouldn't survive. I was going to destroy and burn it all, just like he destroyed their lives, just like he tried to destroy mine.

My stomach felt as if it housed a snake pit, squeezing and slithering as the plane sliced through the lightening sky, inching its way back home, to Simone, to Spots, to danger.

Mia's presence kept me sane. The squeeze of her hand when she felt the tension in my body, the soft, gentle kisses that said it will be ok. Her caring looks and generous nature; it was Mia who got me through that flight without losing my mind, and I loved her for it even more. She understood how deep the pain ran, how urgent the panic was that flooded my very soul. She had known death and loss, and her face held plainly the hurt she held for me until I was prepared to face it and feel it myself.

The plane landed with a screech of the engine as if it too was crying for Simone. We tore through the terminal and passport control, and climbed into the waiting car. Romeo drove. The tyres squealed around corners, like everything around me was in pain, suffering, telling me to run. I should have listened.

The car pulled into the hospital parking bay, but I was

already running, somewhere in there was Simone. She needed me.

The reception area was full. Disease and sickness emanated from half the people in the waiting room, worry and stress from the other half. Murmured conversation and the occasional cough rose above the click-clack of keyboards and ringing phones. I ran to the reception desk and clutched at the plastic counter.

"Simone Moore, please?"

The receptionist looked me up and down through her piggy eyes, set deep in a mound of fat, clucking her tongue. I fought the urge to slap her across the face as she typed on the keyboard looking bored and under appreciated.

"You family?" Her eyes turned to slits as she examined me, her words slurring.

"Yes, I'm family."

She gave me a sceptical look then flashed another look at her screen. "Room 287, third floor to the left. Burns unit."

"Burns unit?" My heart shuddered and stopped, then rebooted with hurtling speed.

She rolled her eyes at me and sighed, "That's what it says here." She waved her hand at the screen as if chasing away a fly.

I was the fly.

"Come on Gabriel, let's go see her." Mia's voice sounded soft and distant. I didn't know how long she'd been standing there.

I turned away and marched to the elevator. Waiting. Grinding my teeth. Feeling my pulse beat throughout my entire body.

The elevator ground to a halt and the doors pulled apart like tearing skin. My feet echoed on the tiled hallway. It felt endless, another tunnel with no light, stuffy with an under-tone of bleach and despair.

Another desk, another nurse, another show of pretence.

"I'm here to see, Simone Moore."

"Are you family?"

"Yes."

The nurse looked me up and down, taking in my weary appearance. Her face was lined and coarse, a testament to the horrors she had witnessed throughout her career. She was gentle under all those furrows, her eyes sad and full of compassion.

"Let me get the doctor for you."

She disappeared behind a door and, once again, there was Mia's touch. Her hand laced into mine and squeezed, willing me to part with some of my tension, some of my fear. But I couldn't, not until I had answers. Not until I saw Simone.

The doctor's face broke into a smile even as she approached. It was practiced and fake, and I hated it. Her white coat was neatly pressed and she nodded to the nurse as they broke apart.

"Hello, I am Doctor DeMar. Please sit down."

"No. I want to see Simone." The doctor stilled for a second then nodded.

"I'm sure she's looking forward to a visit from some family, Mr...?"

"Gabriel."

"Gabriel. I just want to prepare you."

I sucked in a deep breath, settling the bile that rose in my stomach. I didn't move. Silence filled the empty room.

"Follow me," The doctor relented, "But only one of you."

"Send her my love." Mia released my hand and retreated to the tired looking couch in the small waiting area.

The doctor spoke as we walked down another narrow corridor, "Miss Moore sustained third, second, and first degree burns along most of her body. The worst being on her face, hands and the upper torso," Her voice was monotonous and professional as if she was giving a financial report, "We sedated her and she has been sleeping through most of the pain. We cleaned and sterilised her wounds, and she's comfortable for now." She paused, perhaps thinking I needed time to digest. But all she was giving me were words, words that didn't mean a thing until I could piece it all together with my eyes. At my silence she continued, "She will need surgery, skin grafts. Right now, we are taking it one day at a time."

"I want to see her."

"She'll need a lot of support throughout her recovery…"

"Now." The doctor gestured to a door on my right.

"Through that door is a change room. You'll find a gown, gloves, a hair net and a mask. The nurse will help you."

"Thank you, but I've been dressing myself since I was three years old."

"That may be so, Gabriel, but our main concern at the moment is preventing infection. With so much skin exposed…"

"Why are you letting me see her?" I interrupted the doctor mid speech.

"Please follow all the instructions as you undress. Once you're dressed, Ruth will take you through to see her."

Her aversion to my question sent my heart plummeting. I charged into the room already ripping my clothes off.

The nurse, who waited for me in the sterile room, froze for a moment, then her eyes smiled at me beyond her mask, "You must be Gabriel; Simone will be so happy to see you."

I followed Ruth's tedious instructions, my palms feeling too sweaty in the gloves, my body too hot in the gown.

When I was dressed and sterile, Ruth swiped her keycard across the card reader and pushed through the adjoining door. As I made to move into the room, Ruth touched my arm ever so lightly and looked into my eyes, "Be gentle Gabriel." She patted my arm and released me. I stood for a second considering her words and stepped into Simone's room.

I looked at the body on the bed and my heart stumbled. Simone's face and arms were bandaged. The bandages looked too white against the faded, greying sheets that have been washed too many times.

I edged closer to the bed, seeking her face; bandages hid the entire right side, red angry skin edged the dressing. Singed hair poked from between the wraps, completely gone in places. What I did see of her face seemed suddenly too old, too haggard. The joy and happiness charred away by the inferno. She looked too small, too frail, too broken.

"Simone?" I called to her as I approached the bed.

She answered with a garbled moan.

I turned to the nurse, "Can I touch her? Can she hear me?"

"She can hear you alright, but her throat was singed. She inhaled a lot of smoke so she has trouble talking."

I nodded.

I dragged the chair next to the bed, my heart tripping and chugging. I clenched my jaw and lay my hand on Simone's. I almost thought I could feel her flinch. A blackened finger peeked from beyond the bandage.

"Hey, I'm here," I looked at her, and her body shifted in the bed. Her left eye opened into a thin slit, and her lips tipped slightly upwards.

"Never thought seeing my ugly mug would bring anyone such happiness," I brushed my hands along my face.

"Can you tell me what happened? Do you remember anything?" Her eye opened a little larger and it floated about the room, flicking from my face, to her hand, to the nurse and back again.

"You don't worry about a thing. I'll have them move you to the private hospital in the city. You'll get the best care there is. We'll rebuild..." my voice felt strangled as I watched her face grimace.

"Don't worry. I'll look after you, just like you looked after me," I choked on my words, "I promise."

I could feel the tears well in my eyes and the anger fuel beneath my skin. More promises. How many more was I going to have to make, how many was I going to be able to keep?

I sat for a while, watching her breathe, watching her fight. My heart beat trying to match the beeping of the machines around the bed.

I scanned the room, it was devoid of any colour, decoration, or hope. Maybe white was the colour of healing, but it just felt empty, like a tomb. Everything was too clean and sterile, sparse and functional. Depressing.

"You're going to have to leave now, we need to change her dressings and she needs to rest," An agonised moan leaked in from an adjacent room. I clenched my fists into the sheets and slammed my eyes shut wishing I was anywhere but here.

"Sir."

I looked up at the nurse who was now standing a foot away from me, "I'm not leaving her."

She just smiled from behind her mask and approached, her hand landing on my arm, "You can't help her Gabriel. If you stay while we change her, you increase the chance of infection," her hand squeezed my arm, "The best way is for you to go now."

I rubbed my hand over my face and nodded. Her gentle touch fell away.

"See you soon, Simone. I'll be back later. Mia sends her love."

At my words her eye flew open and her fingers searched for my hand.

"Watch...For...Mia..." her voice was hoarse and raspy, and she coughed struggling with the words. The heart rate monitor exploded into life, the beeps chasing one another.

"Of course I will watch out for her, I won't let anything

happen to her. I promise," I gave her a waning smile that I hoped she noticed behind my masked face. The crazed beating of her heart screamed in the room.

"I'll be back." I called over the noise.

"Gabriel, time to go."

I watched Simone's face, her wide eye, her stiff body. The pain drifting away as the nurse plunged a dose of morphine into her IV.

As I left the room, I wondered what spooked her. What did she know? And why was Mia in trouble?

Mia.

My heart wobbled. I had left her alone. Again. I tore the gown and mask away as I sprinted out of Simone's room and into the waiting area.

Mia sat in a stream of sunlight that fell through the book sized window. The single ray played and filtered through her hair and coated her honeyed skin. She looked up from her magazine when she saw me, her eyes growing wide as I ran to her. Into her.

I hooked my arms around her and pulled her to me, allowing my soul to shatter against her body.

"Gabriel?" She held me as I took her warmth and sucked it into myself.

"We need to go. I need to talk to Salvatore." I pushed away the pain, the anguish, and the anger, and buried it deep beneath layer after layer of unresolved issues and undealt with feelings.

I pulled away and snatched her wrist, yanking her behind me.

I stopped at the nurses' station, "Who do I need to speak to about moving Simone Moore into St. Martin Memorial Hospital?" The nurse looked at me, the compassion filling her face hiding something else.

"You can talk to Doctor DeMar about that, and she can

fill in transfer papers. But she won't, not for a few weeks anyway."

"Why not?"

"With burns like the one's Simone sustained, the risk of infection is very high. Moving her now could kill her. I know you want what's best for her, but she is getting the best possible care, I can assure you." The nurse's fingers twitched, as if she thought of moving her hand, then changed her mind, "Simone has a long road to recovery ahead of her. She is very lucky to have you." Although her smile was tainted in sadness, it was genuine.

I sucked in a deep breath and nodded then turned down the hall, dragging Mia along with me.

"Gabriel, slow down."

I ignored her and ploughed through the entrance and into the waiting car, "Take us to Sin. Now."

~∞~

Music poured from the speakers. Shining red and pink lights cast beautiful, swirling patterns across the stage and beamed off the poles.

As we entered, three girls were climbing onto the different stages and gripping their poles. The music began to pound and the women danced. I didn't have to time look; I didn't need to. I've seen it all before.

I turned to Mia who seemed mesmerised by the dancers. I turned to Romeo, "Don't leave her side."

Then to Mia, "Enjoy the show, I'll find you after I'm done with Salvatore." She just nodded as if in a trance watching the women's hips move and breasts bounce. If it wasn't for the kind of day I was having, I would have been very turned on.

I burst into the office. Salvatore sat behind the desk, his face flushed and his chest rising and falling in shallow breaths. His eyes flew open and his head fell back into the seat.

"Do you need me to leave?" I looked him straight in the eyes, and he clenched his jaw, exhaling a breath.

"You're done, Amber." He shifted in the chair. A moment later the petite blonde appeared from beneath the table and wiped her mouth with the back of her hand. Her eyes shot to me and she straightened, her bare breasts bouncing as her hand shot to cover them.

"Sorry boss." She hung her head.

"*You* have nothing to be sorry about, Amber, just make sure he pays you."

Her cheeks flushed red, "Salvatore doesn't need to pay me." A delighted grin crossed her face, and I grimaced internally.

"Get out," Her face fell and she flitted out of the room.

"I thought we talked about this."

"I can't stop her if she wants to—"

"Don't fuck with me today," I cut him off.

He held up his hands and then adjusted his pants, pulling up the zip.

"Tell me what you know about Simone."

Salvatore sighed, "Someone broke in. They were looking for something." We exchanged a knowing look, "When they didn't find anything, they beat her."

"How do you know?"

"Her legs are full of bruises and she was missing a tooth. You don't get that from being in a fire."

My fists clenched against my legs as rage built inside of me. I was too busy looking at burns to search for other injures.

"They threw her upstairs and set the place alight."

"And the dogs?"

"That's where they started the fire."

I hung my head thinking of all the howls, the singed skin,

the desperate growls and shrieks as the animals burned. I thought about Spots and my heart chilled.

"They found her downstairs. She'd tried to rescue the dogs, most were too far gone when she got to them, and the others ran around like crazy things and spread the fire. When the firefighters got there, it was an inferno. They barely managed to get her out, she was fighting for those fucking mutts."

"Those mutts were her family!" I screamed at him, slicing the air with my fist. Feeling the need to stroke Spots' back or scratch his long snout.

"Yeah, right. Sorry."

"Do we know who did this?"

"Emilio."

"Have you found him yet?"

"He's a fucking ghost. No sign of him, no clues, no threads, no loose ends."

"Well, maybe you'd find something if you weren't spending all day getting your cock sucked," I slammed the table with my hand and, for the first time since the beginning of our relationship, I thought I saw Salvatore scared. Truly terrified. Of me. I clenched my jaw as we locked eyes.

"I want him found. No more casualties. This ends now."

Salvatore was already out of his chair and nearing the door.

"Yes boss." He closed the door behind him as he left.

I leaned against the table, clutching its lip, trying to calm my galloping heart, and steady my shivering hands when the door opened and Mia stepped inside, allowing the music to crash into the room.

"Come on, you need to rest." She reached out and I took her hand, her warmth calming me as she guided us through the club and into the hidden corridor that led to the private elevator bank.

The elevator flew to the penthouse and pinged open. Mia steered me through the rooms, bypassing all distractions.

My mind was frayed with worry and anger, distrust and despair as she unclasped my belt and undid my jeans allowing them to slip to my knees. She pushed me onto the bed and removed them throwing them onto the floor. She tapped my arms and I lifted them over my head, allowing her to peel the shirt away from me. I crawled up to the pillow and watched as she unzipped her boots and threw them off, shedding her skirt and shirt, and removing her bra. She crawled onto the bed, her body gluing itself to mine. And like always, she was a balm, soothing and warm as I drifted off to sleep.

The morning felt stark still, the branches of sunlight that seeped in under the door felt harsh and unwelcome. I stretched seeking Mia's warmth. Her side of the bed was empty. I groaned and ran my hands over my face, brushing away sleep and disappointment.

I checked the bedside clock. 11.14 a.m.

Shit.

I bolted up in the bed. I haven't slept that long since that first night at Simone's. Simone.

I jumped up from the bed and opened the curtains. Sunlight spilt into the room. I scanned it for signs of Mia. She was gone.

I walked into the spacious lounge and kitchen area. The curtains covering the floor to ceiling windows were drawn open, and the room felt too white, too bright.

There were no signs of life; no warmth, no smell of coffee or lingering perfume.

"Mia?" I called out. The silence answered in its thundering voice. I shuddered.

"Mia?" Nothing.

I grabbed the receiver and called down stairs to Salvatore's office.

"Morning Boss,"

"Where's Mia?"

"Mia? She came down a couple of hours ago, said you were sleeping and not to disturb you."

"Where'd she go?"

"I don't know."

"And you just fucking let her go?"

"Romeo's with her."

I could feel my pulse slow at the words, "Get a hold of him! Did I have any calls?"

"Just the hospital."

"When? What did they say?"

"They were wondering if you were coming—"

"When did they call?"

"A couple of hours ago."

"Why the fuck didn't you wake me?"

"Mia said—"

"Since when does Mia speak for me? Since when do you take orders from her?"

"Sorry boss I just thought—"

"No, you didn't! I'll be down in ten, have a car ready for me." I hung up, my body shaking with fury. Mia will have to be dealt with later. For now, she was safe—from Emilio and, more importantly, from me. I didn't like the fact that the hospital called.

I splashed water on my face and brushed my teeth, dressed and headed out. My head was swimming with thoughts and drowning in worry I pretended I didn't feel.

I drove too fast and broke too hard. The engine whizzed and complained as I switched it off and made my way into the hospital.

I hurried to the third floor and was greeted by the same

nurse from the previous day. She seemed to have aged in the last twenty-four hours, and I wondered if there was a time when compassion didn't weigh so heavily on her, when the suffering of others didn't bury itself so deeply under her skin.

She gave me a small smile, just a flutter of her lips and my heart jolted. Something was wrong.

Doctor LeMar walked into the room and greeted me, her face expressionless, "Gabriel, so nice to see you."

"How's Simone?"

"Would you like to sit down?"

"No."

The doctor cocked her head and nodded slightly, her lips stretching into a thin line, "I'm afraid I have some bad news. Her condition worsened overnight."

"Just tell me."

The doctor sighed and the stress she carried with her shifted to me as she spoke. I remember watching her lips move but only catching snippets of words; like pulmonary and cardiac failure; given her age and burn area; fighter, just keeping her comfortable. *Goodbye.*

The words floated around me like a cloud until there was only silence. All I could hear was the crack as my world begun to splinter.

"Gabriel?"

"What?" I shook myself from my daze.

"Would you like to say goodbye?"

"No, that's not good enough. There must be something you can do for her."

"Gabriel, there's nothing to do."

"I'm going to move her to a better hospital, get a second opinion. You can't just give up." My voice rose and my anger took hold of me, lashing at the doctor.

She took a small step back, and a pang of guilt shot through me.

"Gabriel," Her avid eyes stared fixedly into mine, and she reached, placing her hand gently on my forearm. "Gabriel," She gave me a waning smile, "There's nothing more that can be done, not by us or anyone else. Take this time to be with her."

I nodded, deflating. My shoulders fell forward as the anger fell from me like a winter's coat.

"Are you ready?"

My heart lurched at the question. *No,* "Yes."

The doctor lead me to Simone's room, bypassing the dressing room. I gave her a questioning look, "There's no need for that anymore."

I clenched my teeth and nodded as the doctor pushed through the door.

The heads looked up. About ten of them, maybe more. They surrounded her like a protective barrier. From me?

I recognised Alex. Tears ran down her ashen face in long, steady rivulets. The others were smiling. It was forced and anxious, and they were talking to Simone. I had no idea if she could hear any of them. But I was glad that she wasn't alone. I was glad that she was loved by at least a few people in this godforsaken pit.

I remained on the periphery, letting them have their time. Letting her enjoy their company. Really, if I am being honest with myself, I stayed so far away because I didn't want to see her, I didn't want to remember her as this broken, blackened thing with tubes and machines keeping her alive. I wanted the bright smiles and the warm hugs, the way she always smelt like wet dog and how she always had a kind word. My heart chugged with despair.

They murmured and talked to her, and I leaned against the back wall feeling their judgment leak over to my side of the room. I knew Alex never approved of our relationship; I wasn't the kind of stray she thought Simone should adopt.

After a while the doctor came back, "Visiting hours are over."

They stood up in unison and each in turn whispered, kissed, or squeezed what was left of her and shuffled out of the room, their tears sitting on the rims of their eyes waiting to be shed.

"You too."

"I'm staying," I moved away from the wall and sat by Simone. At the sound of my voice her heart rate jumped up, "She needs me."

"I'm afraid—"

"I'm afraid *you* don't understand. I am staying. Call the police if you need to, I'm not leaving."

The doctor studied me for a long while. It reminded me of the night Spots was hurt and the way Simone looked at me, through me, as I refused to leave his side. She nodded stiffly and left the room.

There were so many things I wanted to tell her. How can I thank her for everything she'd done for me, for the kindness she's shown and the courage she displayed? There were not enough words in the dictionary, in this language, in any language.

"I'm sorry," I put my hand on hers. Her body remained still but her heart jolted at my touch, at my voice; the beeping screeching through the heart monitor. Without any warning multiple alarms sounded, various machines burst into life. The room flooded with nurses and doctors that pushed me out of the way. Their faces drawn but resigned. I looked at the clock. Only minutes left, only seconds.

Chaos.

Calling.

Chirping.

Screaming.

Flatline.

And just like that, I'd lost a mother all over again.

I knew Doctor LeMar was speaking because I saw her lips move. We were moving but I didn't feel my legs walk; maybe I was floating, maybe I was sinking. Then there were the faces of the others; they were hugging and crying and staring, and I didn't belong. I never belonged.

I was back in my car and it was moving, floating through traffic—the tyres spinning, the engine revving all on their own because I wasn't there. Not really.

Then I could feel the breeze, shade covered my face through the strong sunlight. The bench was sturdy beneath me, somehow holding me up. But there was no Alice, there was no Simone, and all I felt was a great emptiness—a gaping black hole of sadness. I sat in a pool of regret, saturated by my sins and my guilt. It was all my fault. Just another promise I couldn't keep, another life I couldn't save, another shining light that I brought to an end. I was a destroyer of worlds and the creator of misery.

And I would bring my gift to Emilio. I would break and destroy everything he held dear.

All I had to do was find him.

I sucked in a long, hard breath, burying all the pain and all the anguish; and holding on to the anger, the hatred, and the bitterness. I would need them. For later.

Right now, I had to deal with the living.

To be continued...

ACKNOWLEDGMENTS

A Word from Jane:

I would like to start by thanking you, the reader, so much for reading! If you enjoyed the story, please leave a review and recommend the book to any friend you think would love Gabriel's story. You will have my eternal love and gratitude. Even a few short words go a long way.

As always, I would love to thank my wonderful friend and beta Dawn, her enthusiasm knows no boundaries, her genuine love for books, reading, and helping authors is contagious and humbling. I have loved having her in my corner. Thank you.

To all my other betas and C/Ps your input and critiques have been invaluable, without you Gabriel would not have been where he is today.

ABOUT THE AUTHOR

Jane Wynters doesn't quite know how to answer the question of "where are you from?" She's moved from place to place like a snowflake on the wind always searching for a safe place to land. She loves meeting new people and exploring new places. She loves reading, writing and conjuring new worlds from her imagination. Coffee is at the top of her food pyramid and she is fluent in three languages, her favourite being sarcasm.

Want to know more about the author and keep in touch? Get snippets of up coming books and have a bit of twisted fun?

Come join me in Wonderland…